W9-AKV-086

UNCLE WIGGILY'S ADVENTURES

Other Books by Howard R. Garis:

UNCLE WIGGILY BEDTIME STORIES
Uncle Wiggily's Adventures
Uncle Wiggily's Travels
Uncle Wiggily's Fortune
Uncle Wiggily's Automobile
Uncle Wiggily at the Seashore
Uncle Wiggily's Airship
Uncle Wiggily in the Country
Uncle Wiggily in the Woods
Uncle Wiggily on the Farm
Uncle Wiggily's Journey
Uncle Wiggily's Rheumatism
Uncle Wiggily and Baby Bunty
Uncle Wiggily in Wonderland
Uncle Wiggily in Fairyland
Uncle Wiggily and Mother Hubbard
Uncle Wiggily and the Birds

UNCLE WIGGILY ANIMAL STORIES
Sammie and Susie Littletail
Johnnie and Billie Bushytail
Lulu, Alice, and Jimmie Wibblewobble
Jackie and Peetie Bow-Wow
Buddy and Brighteyes Pigg
Joie, Tommie and Kittie Kat
Charlie and Arabella Chick
Neddie and Beckie Stubtail
Bully and Bawly No-Tail
Nannie and Billie Wagtail
Jollie and Jillie Longtail
Jacko and Jumpo Kinkytail
Curly and Floppy Twistytail
Toodle and Noodle Flattail
Dottie and Willie Flufftail
Dickie and Nellie Fliptail
Woodie and Waddie Chuck
Bobby and Betty Ringtail

Uncle Wiggily's Story Book
Uncle Wiggily's Picture Book

UNCLE WIGGILY'S ADVENTURES

Howard R. Garis

ÆGYPAN PRESS

1912

Special thanks to Clare Boothby, David Newman, Emmy and the
Online Distributed Proofreading Team (which can be found at
http://www.pgdp.net).

Uncle Wiggily's Adventures
A publication of
ÆGYPAN PRESS

www.aegypan.com

Story I

UNCLE WIGGILY STARTS OFF

*U*ncle Wiggily Longears, the nice old gentleman rabbit, hopped out of bed one morning and started to go to the window, to see if the sun was shining. But, no sooner had he stepped on the floor, than he cried out:

"Oh! Ouch! Oh, dear me and a potato pancake! Oh, I believe I stepped on a tack! Sammie Littletail must have left it there! How careless of him!"

You see this was the same Uncle Wiggily, of whom I have told you in the Bedtime Books — the very same Uncle Wiggily. He was an Uncle to Sammie and Susie Littletail, the rabbit children, and also to Billie and Johnnie Bushytail, the squirrel boys, and to Alice and Lulu and Jimmie Wibblewobble, the duck children, and I have written for you, books about all those characters. Now I thought I would write something just about Uncle Wiggily himself, though of course I'll tell you what all his nephews and nieces did, too.

Well, when Uncle Wiggily felt that sharp pain, he stood still for a moment, and wondered what could have happened.

"Yes, I'm almost sure it was a tack," he said. "I must pick it up so no one else will step on it."

So Uncle Wiggily looked on the floor, but there was no tack there, only some crumbs from a sugar cookie that Susie Littletail had been eating the night before, when her uncle had told her a go-to-sleep story.

"Oh, I know what it was; it must have been my rheumatism that gave me the pain!" said the old gentleman rabbit as he looked for his red, white and blue crutch, striped like a barber pole. He found it under the bed, and then he managed to limp to the window. Surely enough, the sun was shining.

"I'll certainly have to do something about this rheumatism," said Uncle Wiggily as he carefully shaved himself by looking in the glass. "I guess I'll see Dr. Possum."

So after breakfast, when Sammie and Susie had gone to school, Dr. Possum was telephoned for, and he called to see Uncle Wiggily.

"Ha! Hum!" exclaimed the doctor, looking very wise. "You have the rheumatism very bad, Mr. Longears."

"Why, I knew that before you came," said the old gentleman rabbit, blinking his eyes. "What I want is something to cure it."

"Ha! Hum!" said Dr. Possum, again looking very wise. "I think you need a change of air. You must travel about. Go on a journey, get out and see strange birds, and pick the pretty flowers. You don't get exercise enough."

"Exercise enough!" cried Uncle Wiggily. "Why, my goodness me sakes alive and a bunch of lilacs! Don't I play checkers almost every night with Grandfather Goosey Gander?"

"That is not enough," said the doctor, "you must travel here and there, and see things."

"Very well," said Uncle Wiggily, "then I will travel. I'll pack my valise at once, and I'll go off and seek my fortune, and maybe, on the way, I can lose this rheumatism."

So the next day Uncle Wiggily started out with his crutch, and his valise packed full of clean clothes, and something in it to eat.

"Oh, we are very sorry to have you go, dear uncle," said Susie Littletail, "but we hope you'll come back good and strong."

"Thank you," said Uncle Wiggily, as he kissed the two rabbit children and their mamma, and shook hands with Papa Littletail. Then off the old gentleman bunny hopped with his crutch.

Well, he went along for quite a distance, over the hills, and down the road, and through the woods, and, as the sun got higher and warmer, his rheumatism felt better.

"I do believe Dr. Possum was right!" said Uncle Wiggily. "Traveling is just the thing for me," and he felt so very jolly that he whistled a little tune about a peanut wagon, which roasted lemonade, and boiled and frizzled Easter eggs that Mrs. Cluk-Cluk laid.

"Ha! Where are you going?" suddenly asked a voice, as Uncle Wiggily finished the tune.

"I'm going to seek my fortune," replied Uncle Wiggily. "Who are you, pray?"

"Oh, I'm a friend of yours," said the voice, and Uncle Wiggily looked all around, but he couldn't discover anyone.

"But where are you?" the puzzled old gentleman rabbit wanted to know. "I can't see you."

"No, and for a very good reason," answered the voice. "You see I have very weak eyes, and if I came out in the sun, without my smoked glasses on, I might get blind. So I have to hide down in this hollow stump."

"Then put on your glasses and come out where I can see you," invited the old gentleman rabbit, and all the while he was trying to remember where he had heard that voice before. At first he thought it might be Grandfather Goosey Gander, or Uncle Butter, the goat, yet it didn't sound like either of them.

"I have sent my glasses to the store to be fixed, so I can't wear them and come out," went on the voice. "But if you are seeking your fortune I know the very place where you can find it."

"Where?" asked Uncle Wiggily, eagerly.

"Right down in this hollow stump," was the reply. "There are all kinds of fortunes here, and you may take any kind you like Mr. Longears."

"Ha! That is very nice," thought the rabbit. "I have not had to travel far before finding my fortune. I wonder if there is a cure for rheumatism in that stump, too?" So he asked about it.

"Of course, your rheumatism can be cured in here," came the quick answer. "In fact, I guarantee to cure any disease — measles, chicken-pox, mumps and even toothache. So if you have any friends you want cured send them to me."

"I wish I could find out who you were," spoke the rabbit. "I seem to know your voice, but I can't think of your name."

"Oh, you'll know me as soon as you see me," said the voice. "Just hop down inside this hollow stump, and your fortune is as good as made, and your rheumatism will soon be gone. Hop right down."

Well, Uncle Wiggily didn't like the looks of the black hole down inside the stump, and he peered into it to see what he could see, but it was so black that all he could make out was something like a lump of coal.

"Well, Dr. Possum said I needed to have a change of scene, and some adventures," said the rabbit, "so I guess I'll chance it. I'll go down, and perhaps I may find my fortune."

Then, carefully holding his crutch and his satchel, Uncle Wiggily hopped down inside the stump. He felt something soft, and furry, and fuzzy, pressing close to him, and at first he thought he had bumped into Dottie or Willie Lambkin.

But then, all of a sudden, a harsh voice cried out:

"Ha! Now I have you! I was just wishing someone would come along with my dinner, and you did! Get in there, and see if you can find your fortune, Uncle Wiggily!" And with that what should happen but that big, black bear, who had been hiding in the stump, pushed Uncle Wiggily into a dark closet, and locked the door! And there the poor rabbit was, and the bear was getting ready to eat him up.

But don't worry, I'll find a way to get him out, and in case we have ice cream pancakes for supper I'll tell you, in the next story, how Uncle Wiggily got out of the bear's den, and how he went fishing — I mean Uncle Wiggily went fishing, not the bear.

Story II

UNCLE WIGGILY GOES FISHING

At first, after he found himself shut up in the bear's dark closet, where we left him in the story before this, poor Uncle Wiggily didn't know what to think. He just sat there, on the edge of a chair, and he tried to look around, and see something, but it was too black, so he couldn't.

"Perhaps this is only a joke," thought the old gentleman rabbit, "though I never knew a black bear to joke before. But perhaps it is. I'll ask him."

So Uncle Wiggily called out:

"Is this a joke, Mr. Bear?"

"Not a bit of it!" was the growling answer. "You'll soon see what's going to happen to you! I'm getting the fire ready now."

"Getting the fire ready for what; the adventure, or for my fortune?" asked the rabbit, for he still hoped the bear was only joking with him.

"Ready to cook you!" was the reply. "That's what the fire is for!" and the bear gnashed his teeth together something terrible, and, with his sharp claws, he clawed big splinters off the stump, and with them he started the fire in the stove, with the splinters, I mean, not his claws.

The blazing fire made it a little brighter in the hollow stump, which was the black bear's den, and Uncle Wiggily could look out of a crack in the door, and see what a savage fellow the shaggy bear was. You see, that bear just hid in the stump, waiting for helpless animals to come along, and then he'd trick them into jumping down inside of it, and there wasn't a word of truth about him having sore eyes, or about him having to wear dark spectacles, either.

"Oh, my! I guess this is the end of my adventures," thought the rabbit. "I should have been more careful. Well, I wish I could see Sammie and Susie before he eats me, but I'm afraid I can't. I shouldn't have jumped down here."

But as Uncle Wiggily happened to think of Sammie Littletail, the boy rabbit, he also thought of something else. And this was that Sammie had put something in the old gentleman rabbit's valise that morning, before his uncle had started off.

"If you ever get into trouble, Uncle Wiggily," Sammie had said, "this may come in useful for you." Uncle Wiggily didn't look at the time to see what it was that his nephew put in the valise, but he made up his mind he would do so now. So he opened his satchel, and there, among other things, was a long piece of thin, but strong rope. And pinned to it was a note which read:

"Dear Uncle Wiggily. This is good to help you get out of a window, in case of fire."

"My goodness!" exclaimed Uncle Wiggily, "that's fine. There the bear is making a fire to cook me, and with this rope I can get away from it. Now if there's only a window in this closet I'm all right."

So he looked, and sure enough there was a window. And with his crutch Uncle Wiggily raised it. Then he threw out his satchel, and he tied the rope to a hook on the windowsill, and, being a strong old gentleman, he crawled out of the window, and slid down the cord.

And Uncle Wiggily got out just as the bear opened the closet door to grab him, and put him in the pot, and when the savage black creature saw his fine rabbit dinner getting away he was as angry as anything, really he was.

"Here! Come back here!" cried the bear, but of course Uncle Wiggily knew better than to come back. He slid down the rope to the ground, and then he cut off as much of the rope as he could, and put it in his pocket, for he didn't know when he might need it again. Then, catching up his valise, he ran on and on, before the bear could get to him.

It was still quite a dark place in which Uncle Wiggily was, for you see he was underground, down by the roots of the stump. But he looked ahead and he saw a little glimmer of light, and then he knew he could get out.

Limping on his crutch, and carrying his valise, he went on and on, and pretty soon he came out of a dark cave and found himself on the bank of a nice little brook, that was running over mossy, green stones.

"Ha! This is better than being in a bear's den!" exclaimed the old gentleman rabbit. "My, I was so frightened that I forgot about my rheumatism hurting me. That was an adventure all right, and Sammie was a good boy to think of that strong cord. Now what shall I do next?"

Well, Uncle Wiggily sat down on the bank of the brook, and he looked in the water. Then he happened to see a fish jump up to catch a bug, so he said to himself:

"I guess I will go fishing, just for fun. But if I do happen to catch any fish I'll put them right back in the water again. For I don't need any fish, as I have some lettuce and cabbage sandwiches, and some peanut-butter cakes, that Susie's mamma put up in a cracker-box for me."

Well, Uncle Wiggily looked in his valise, to make sure his lunch was safe, and then, taking a bent pin from under his vest, he fastened it to a part of the string Sammie had given him. Then he fastened the string to a pole, and he was ready to fish, but he needed something to make the fishes bite — that is, bite the pinhook, not bite him, you know.

"Oh, I guess they'll like a bit of sweet cracker," Uncle Wiggily thought; so he put some on the end of the pin-hook, and threw it toward the water.

It fell in with a splash, and made a lot of little circles, like ring-around the rosies, and the rabbit sat there looking at them, sort of nodding, and half asleep and wondering what adventure would happen to him next, and where he would stay that night. All of a sudden he felt something tugging at the hook and line.

"Oh, I've got a fish! I've got a fish!" he cried, as he lifted up the pole. Up out of the water with a sizzling rush flew the string and the sweet cracker bait, and the next minute out leaped the big, savage alligator that had escaped from a circus.

"Oh, ho! So you tried to catch me, eh?" the alligator shouted at Uncle Wiggily.

"No — no, if you please," said the rabbit. "I was after fish."

"And I'm after you!" cried the alligator, and, scrambling up the bank, he made a jump for Uncle Wiggily, and with one sweep of his kinky, scaly tail he flopped and he threw the old gentleman rabbit and his crutch and valise right up into a big tree that grew near the brook.

"There you'll stay until I get ready to eat you!" exclaimed the alligator, as he stood up on the end of his tail under the tree, and opened his mouth as wide as he could so that if Uncle Wiggily fell down he'd fall into it, just like down a funnel, you know.

Well, the poor gentleman rabbit clung to the topmost tree branch, wondering how in the world he was going to escape from the alligator. Oh, it was a dreadful position to be in!

But please don't worry or stay awake over it, for I'll find a way to get him down safely. And in the story after this, if the milkman doesn't leave us sour cream for our lemonade, I'll tell you about Uncle Wiggily and the black crow.

Story III

UNCLE WIGGILY AND THE BLACK CROW

*L*et me see, where did I leave off in the last story? Oh! I remember. It was about Uncle Wiggily Longears being up in the top of the tall tree, and the alligator keeping guard down below, ready to eat him.

Well, the old gentleman rabbit was wondering how he could ever escape, and he felt quite badly about it.

"I guess this is the end of my adventures," he said to himself. "It would have been much better had I stayed at home with Sammie and Susie." And as he thought of the two rabbit children he felt still sadder, and very lonely.

"I wonder if Susie could have put anything in my satchel with which to scare an alligator," thought Uncle Wiggily. "I guess I'll look." So he looked, and what should he find but a bottle of toothache drops. Yes, there it was, and wrapped ground it was a little note Susie had written.

"Dear Uncle Wiggily," she said in the note, "if you ever get the toothache on your travels, this will stop it."

"Ha! That is very kind of Susie, I'm sure," said the rabbit, "but I don't see how that is going to make the alligator go away. And, even if he does go, I wonder how I'm to get down out of this tall tree, with my crutch, my valise and my rheumatism?"

Well, just then the alligator got tired of standing on the end of his tail, with his mouth open, and he began crawling around. Then he thought of what a good supper he was going to have of Uncle Wiggily, and that alligator said:

"I guess I'll sharpen my teeth so I can eat him better," and with that the savage and unpleasant creature began to gnaw on a stone, to sharpen his teeth. Then he stood up on the end of his tail once more, under the tree, and opened his mouth as wide as he could.

"Come on now!" he called to Uncle Wiggily. "Jump down and have it over with."

"Oh, but I don't want to," objected the rabbit.

"You'll have to, whether you want to or not," went on the alligator. "If you don't come down, I'll take my scaly, naily tail, and I'll saw down the tree, and then you'll fall."

"Oh, dear!" exclaimed Uncle Wiggily. "What shall I do?"

Then he happened to think of the bottle of toothache medicine that he held in his hand, and, taking out the cork, he dropped the bottle, medicine and all, right into the open mouth of the alligator, who was again up on his tail.

And the alligator thought it was Uncle Wiggily falling into his jaws, and he shut them quickly like a steel trap and chewed on that bottle of hot toothache drops before he knew what it was.

Well, you can just imagine what happened. The medicine was as hot as pepper and mustard and vinegar and cloves and horse radish all made into one! My! how it did burn that alligator's mouth.

"Oh my! I'm shot! I'm poisoned! I'm bitten by a mosquito! I'm stabbed! I'm all scrambled up" cried the alligator. "Water, water, quick! I must have water!"

Then he gave a big jump, and, with his kinkery-scalery tail, he leaped into a big puddle of water, and went away down in under, out of sight, to cool off his mouth.

"Oh, now is my chance! If I could only get down out of the tree!" exclaimed Uncle Wiggily. "But with my rheumatism I'm afraid I'll fall. Oh dear! What shall I do?"

"Don't be afraid, I'll help you!" exclaimed a kind voice, and then the voice went on: "Caw! Caw! Caw!" and Uncle Wiggily, looking up, saw a big black crow perched on a limb over his head.

"Oh, how do you do!" spoke Uncle Wiggily, making a bow as well as he could. "Can you really help me down?"

"Yes," said the crow, "I can. Wait until I get my market basket. I was just going to the grocery, but I'm in no hurry. I'll save you first."

So that crow flew off, and in a moment he came back with a big basket in its bill.

"Hop in!" the black crow called to Uncle Wiggily, "and I'll fly down to the ground with you, and you can run off before the alligator comes out of the water. I saw what you did to him with those toothache drops, and it served him right. Come on, hop in the basket."

So Uncle Wiggily got in the basket, and the crow, taking the handle in his strong beak, flew safely to the ground with him. And that's how the old gentleman rabbit got down out of the tree, just as I told you he would.

So he and the crow walked on some distance through the woods together, after Uncle Wiggily had picked up his crutch and valise, which had fallen out of the basket, and they got safely away before the alligator came out of the water. And wasn't he the provoked old beastie, though, when he saw that his rabbit supper was gone?

"Where are you going?" asked the crow of Uncle Wiggily, after a bit, when they got to a nice big stone, and sat down for a rest.

"I am seeking my fortune," replied the old gentleman rabbit, "and trying to get better of my rheumatism. Dr. Possum told me to travel, and have adventures, and I've had quite a few already."

"Well, I hope you find your fortune and that it turns out to be a very good one," said the kind crow. "But it is coming on night now. Have you anyplace to stay?"

"No," replied the rabbit, "I haven't. I never thought about that. What shall I do?"

"Oh, don't worry," said the crow. "I'd let you stay in my nest, but it is up a high tree, and you would have trouble climbing in and out. But near my nest-house is an old hollow stump, and you can stay in that very nicely."

"Are there any bears in it?" asked Uncle Wiggily, carefullike.

"Oh, no; not a one. It is very safe."

So the crow showed Uncle Wiggily where the hollow stump was, and he slept there all night, on a soft bed of leaves. And when he awakened in the morning he had breakfast with the crow and once more started off to seek his fortune.

Well, pretty soon, in a short while, not so very long, he came to a little house made of bark, standing in the middle of a deep, dark, dismal woods. And on the door of the house was a sign which read:

"If you want to be surprised, open this door and come in."

"Perhaps I can find my fortune in there, and get rid of the rheumatism," thought Uncle Wiggily, so he hopped forward. And just as he did so he heard a voice calling to him:

"Don't go in! Don't go in there, Uncle Wiggily!"

The rabbit looked up, and saw Johnnie Bushytail, the squirrel boy, waving his paws at him. Well, Uncle Wiggily started to jump back away from the door of the little house, but it was too late. Out came a scraggily-raggily claw, which grabbed him, while a voice cried out:

"Ah, ha! Now I have you! Come right in!"

And then, before you could shake a stick at a bad dog, the door was slammed shut and locked, and there Uncle Wiggily was inside the house, and Johnnie Bushytail was crying outside.

"That's the end of poor Uncle Wiggily!" said Johnnie. But it wasn't. For I'll not leave the old gentleman rabbit alone in the house with that clawy creature. And in the next story, providing our wash lady doesn't put my new straw hat in the soap suds, and take all the color out of the ribbon, I'll tell you about Uncle Wiggily and Fido Flip-Flop.

Story IV

UNCLE WIGGILY AND FIDO FLIP-FLOP

*W*ell, as soon as Uncle Wiggily found himself inside the bear's den – oh, just listen to me! That was in the other story, wasn't it? Yes, we left him in the funny little house in the woods, with the clawy creature grabbing him.

Now, what do you suppose that clawy creature was? Why, a great, big owl, to be sure, with round, staring, yellow eyes, and he had grabbed Uncle Wiggily in his claws, and pulled him inside the house.

"Now, I've got you!" cried the owl. "I was just wishing someone would come along, and you did. Some of my friends are coming to tea this afternoon, and you'll do very nicely made up into sandwiches."

Wasn't that a perfectly dreadful way to talk about our Uncle Wiggily? Well, I guess yes!

"Now you're here, make yourself at home," went on the owl, sarcasticlike, as he locked the front door and put the key in his pocket. "Did you see the sign?"

"Yes," said Uncle Wiggily, "I did. But I don't call it fair. I thought I would find my fortune in here."

"The sign says you'll be surprised, and I guess you are surprised, aren't you?" asked the owl.

"Yes," answered the rabbit, "very much so. But I'd rather have a nice surprise party, with peanuts and lemonade, than this."

"No matter," said the owl, snapping his beak like a pair of shears, "here you are and here you'll stay! My friends will soon arrive. I'll now put the kettle on, to boil for tea."

Well, poor Uncle Wiggily didn't know what to do. He couldn't look in his valise to see if there was anything in it by which he might escape, for he had dropped the satchel outside when the owl grabbed him, and he only had his barber-pole crutch.

"Oh, this is worse and worse!" thought the poor old rabbit.

But listen, Johnnie Bushytail is outside the owl's house, and he's going to do a wonderful trick.

As soon as he saw the door shut on Uncle Wiggily, that brave squirrel boy began to plan how he could save him, and the first thing he did was to gather up a lot of acorns.

Then he perched himself in a tree, right in front of the owl's door, and Johnnie began throwing acorns at it. "Rat-a-tat-tat!" went the acorns on the wooden panels.

"Ha! Those must be my friends!" exclaimed the bad owl, opening the door a little crack so he could peek out, but taking care to stand in front of it, so that Uncle Wiggily couldn't slip out. But, of course, the owl saw no one. "It must have been the wind," he said as he shut the door.

Then Johnnie Bushytail threw some more acorns at the door. "Pitter-patter-patter-pit!" they went, like hailstones in an ice cream can.

"Ah, there are my friends, sure, this time!" thought the owl, and once more he peered out, but no one was there. "It must have been a tree branch hitting against the door," said the owl, as he sharpened a big knife with which to make the sandwiches. Then Johnnie threw some more acorns, and the owl now thought positively his friends were there, and when he opened it and saw no one he was real mad.

"Someone is playing tricks on me!" exclaimed the savage bird. "I'll catch them next time!"

Now this was just what Johnnie Bushytail wanted, so he threw a whole double handful of acorns at the door, and when the owl heard them pattering against the wood he rushed out.

"Now, I've got you!" he cried, but he hadn't, for Johnnie was up a tree. And, for the moment, the owl forgot about Uncle Wiggily, and there the door was wide open.

"Run out, Uncle Wiggily! Run out!" cried Johnnie, and out the old gentleman rabbit hopped, catching up his valise, and away into the woods he ran, with Johnnie scurrying along in the tree tops above him, and laughing at the owl, who flew back to his house, but too late to catch the bunny.

"That's what you get for fooling people so they'll come into your house," called the squirrel boy. "It serves you right, Mr. Owl. Come on, Uncle Wiggily, we'll get away from here."

So they went on together until it was time for Johnnie to go home, and he said he'd tell Uncle Wiggily's friends that he had met the old gentleman rabbit, and that he hadn't found his fortune yet, but that he was looking for it every minute, and had had many adventures.

Well, Uncle Wiggily went on some more, for quite a distance, until it was noon time, and then he sat down in the cool, green woods, where there were some jacks-in-the-pulpit growing near some ferns, and there Uncle Wiggily ate his lunch of lettuce sandwiches, with carrot butter on them, and gnawed on a bit of potato. Just as he was almost through, he heard a rustling in the bushes, and a voice exclaimed:

"Oh, dear!"

"Why, what's the matter?" asked Uncle Wiggily, thinking perhaps an adventure was going to happen to him. "Who are you?"

"Oh, dear!" exclaimed the voice again.

Then, before the old rabbit could jump up and run away, even if he had wanted to, out from under a big bush came a little white poodle dog, with curly, silky hair. He walked right up to Uncle Wiggily, that dog did, and the rabbit wasn't a bit afraid, for the dog wasn't much bigger than he was, and looked very kind.

"What do you want, doggie?" gently asked Uncle Wiggily.

The dog didn't answer, but he gave a little short bark, and then he began turning somersaults. Over and over he went, sometimes backward and sometimes frontward, and sometimes sideways. And when he was finished, he made a low bow, and walked around on his two hind legs, just to show he wasn't proud or stuck up.

"There!" exclaimed the poodle doggie. "Is that worth something to eat, Mr. Rabbit?"

"Indeed it is," answered Uncle Wiggily, "but I would have given you something to eat without you doing all those tricks, though I enjoyed them very much. Where did you learn to do them?"

"Oh, in the circus where I used to be, I always had to do tricks for my dinner," said the doggie.

"What is your name?" asked Uncle Wiggily.

"Fido Flip-Flop," was the answer. "You see they call me that because I turn so many flip-flops," and then Uncle Wiggily gave him some lunch, and told the dog about how he, himself, was traveling all over in search of his fortune.

"Why, that's just what I'm doing, too," exclaimed Fido Flip-Flop. "Suppose we travel together? and maybe we'll each find a fortune."

"That's just what we'll do," agreed Uncle Wiggily.

And then, all of a sudden, before you could open your eyes and shut them again, two savage foxes jumped out from behind a big stump.

"You grab the dog and I'll grab the rabbit," called the biggest fox, and right at Uncle Wiggily and Fido they sprang, gnashing their teeth.

But don't worry. I'll find a way to save them, and if the canary bird doesn't take my lead pencil and stick it in his seed dish I'll tell you in the following story about Uncle Wiggily doing some tricks.

Story V

UNCLE WIGGILY DOES SOME TRICKS

*W*hen those two savage ducks — oh, I mean foxes — when those two savage foxes jumped out of the bushes at Uncle Wiggily Longears and Fido Flip-Flop, as I told you in the other story, the rabbit and the poodle doggie didn't know what in the world to do.

"Run this way!" called Fido, starting off to the left.

"No, hop this way!" said Uncle Wiggily, hopping to the right.

"Stand right where you are!" ordered the two foxes together. And with that one made a grab for Uncle Wiggily. But what did that brave rabbit gentleman do but stick his red-white-and-blue crutch out in front of him, and the fox bit on that instead of on Uncle Wiggily. Right into the crutch the fox's teeth sank, and for a moment Uncle Wiggily was safe. But not for long.

"Ah, you fooled me that time, but now I'll get you!" cried the fox, and, letting go of the crutch, he made another grab for the rabbit.

But at that instant Fido Flip-Flop, who had been jumping about, keeping out of the way of the fox that was after him, cried out quite loudly:

"Look here, everybody but Uncle Wiggily, and, as for you, shut both your eyes tight."

Now the old gentleman rabbit couldn't imagine why he was to shut his eyes tight, but he did so, and then what do you s'pose Fido Flip-Flop did? Why, he began turning somersaults so fast that he looked just like a pinwheel going around, or an automobile tire whizzing along. Faster and faster did Fido Flip-Flop turn around, and then, all of a sudden, he began chasing his tail, making motions just like a merry-go-round in a circus, until those two foxes were fairly dizzy from watching him.

"Stop! Stop!" cried one fox.

"Yes do stop! We're so dizzy that we can't stand up!" cried the other fox, staggering about. "Stop!"

"No, I'll not!" answered Fido Flip-Flop, and he went around faster that ever, faster and faster and faster, until those two bad foxes got so dizzy-izzy that they fell right over on their backs, with their legs sticking straight up in the air like clothes posts, and their tails were wiggling back and forth in the dirt, like dusting brushes. Oh, but they were the dizzy foxes, though.

"Now's your chance! Run! Run! Uncle Wiggily! Run!" called Fido Flip-Flop "Open your eyes and run!"

So the old gentleman rabbit opened his eyes, took up his valise which he had dropped, and, hopping on his crutch, he and the poodle doggie ran on through the woods, leaving the two surprised and disappointed foxes still lying on their backs, wiggling their tails in the dust, and too dizzy, from having watched Fido Flip-Flop do somersaults, and chase his tail, to be able to get up.

"Why did you want me to shut my eyes?" asked Uncle Wiggily, when they were so far away from the foxes that there was no more danger.

"That was so *you* wouldn't get dizzy from watching me do the flip-flops," answered the doggie. "My, but that was a narrow escape, though. Have you had many adventures like that since you started out to seek your fortune?"

"Yes, several," answered the rabbit. "But turning flip-flops is a very good thing to know how to do. I wonder if you could teach me, so that when anymore foxes or alligators chase me I can make them dizzy by turning around? Can you teach me?"

"I'm sure I can," said Fido. "Here, this is the way to begin," and he did some flip-flops slow and easylike. Then Uncle Wiggily tried them, and, though he couldn't do them very well at first, he practiced until he was quite good at it. Then Fido showed him how to stand on one ear, and wiggle the other, and how to blink his eyes while standing on the end of his little tail, and then Uncle Wiggily thought of a new trick, all by himself.

"I'll stick my crutch in the ground, like a clothes pole," he said to Fido, "and then I'll hop up on it and sing a song," which he did, singing a song that went like this:

"Did you ever see a rabbit
 Do a flipper-flopper-flap?
 If not just kindly watch me,
 As I wear my baseball cap.

"It's very strange, some folks may say,
 And also rather funny,

To see a kinky poodle dog
Play with a flip-flop bunny.

"But we are on our travels,
Adventures for to seek,
We may find one, or two, or three,
'Most any day next week."

And then Uncle Wiggily hopped down, and waved both ears backward and forward, and made a low bow to a make-believe crowd of people, only, of course, there were none there.

"Fine! Fine!" cried Fido Flip-Flop. "That's better than I did when I was in the circus. Now I'll tell you what let's do."

"What?" asked Uncle Wiggily.

"Let's go around and give little shows and entertainments, for little folks to see," went on the poodle doggie. "I can turn flip-flops, and you can stand on your head on your crutch, and sing a song, and then we'll take up a collection. I'll pass my hat, and perhaps we may make our fortune – who knows?"

"Who, indeed?" said Uncle Wiggily. "We'll do it."

So off they started together to give a little show, and make some money, and, as they went on through the woods, they practiced doing the tricks Uncle Wiggily had learned.

Well, in a little while, not so very long, they came to a nice place in the forest – an open place where no trees grew.

"Here is a good spot for our show," said Uncle Wiggily.

"But there is no one to see us do the tricks," objected Fido.

"Oh, yes, there are some ants, and an angle worm, and a black bug and a grasshopper," said Uncle Wiggily. "They will do to start on, and after they see us do the tricks they'll tell other folks, and we'll have quite a crowd."

So they started in to do their tricks. Fido turned a lot of flip-flops, and Uncle Wiggily did a dance on the end of his crutch, and sang a song about a monkey-doodle, which the angle worm said was just fine, being quite cute, and the grasshopper made believe play a fiddle with his two hind legs, scratching one on the other, and making lovely music.

But, all of a sudden, just as Uncle Wiggily was standing on his left ear, and wiggling his feet in the air, which is a very hard trick for a rabbit, what should happen but that out of the woods sprang two boys.

"There's the dog! Grab him!" cried one boy. "Never mind about the rabbit! Get the trick dog!" And the boys rushed right up, knocking Uncle Wiggily down, and grabbing Fido Flip-Flop. And they started off through the woods with him, while Uncle Wiggily cried out for them to come back. But they wouldn't.

Now please don't feel badly, for I'm going to tell you in the next story how Uncle Wiggily saved Fido, and also how the rabbit went to Arabella Chick's surprise party — that is I will if our automobile doesn't turn upside down, and break my ice cream cone.

Story VI

UNCLE WIGGILY AT THE PARTY

*W*ell, when Uncle Wiggily Longears found that the elephant wouldn't get off his trunk — oh, listen to me! What I meant to say was, that when Uncle Wiggily saw those two boys running off with Fido Flip-Flop, the little trick dog, as I told you about in the story before this, the old gentleman rabbit was so surprised at first that he didn't know what to do.

"Won't you please come back with that little doggie?" begged Uncle Wiggily, but the bad boys kept right on. I guess they knew how smart Fido was, and they wanted to get up a show with him. Anyhow, they kept on running through the woods, holding him tightly in their arms.

"Oh, dear! This is terrible!" exclaimed Uncle Wiggily. "I'll never get any good fortune if Fido has such bad luck. And it was partly my fault, too, for if we hadn't been doing tricks, we would have heard these boys coming, and could have run away. Well, now I must save Fido."

So Uncle Wiggily sat down on a stump, and thought, and thought, and thought of all the plans he could think of, to save the doggie from the two boys, and at last he decided the only way to do was to scare them.

"Then they'll drop Fido, and run away," said the old gentleman rabbit. "Let me see, how can I scare them? I know, I'll make believe I'm a tiger!"

So what did that brave Uncle Wiggily do? but go to a mud hole, and with his crutch dipped into the mud, he made himself all striped over like a tiger that you see in a circus. Oh, he was a most ferocious sight when he finished decorating himself! Then he hid his satchel in the bushes, and he started off on a short cut through the woods, to get ahead of the boys. Faster and faster through the woods went Uncle Wiggily, and he looked so peculiarly terrifying that all the animals who saw him were scared out of their wits, and one old blue-jay bird was so frightened that he wiggled his tail up and down, and hid his head in a hollow tree.

Well, by and by, after a while, Uncle Wiggily got to a place in the woods where he knew those boys, with Fido Flip-Flop, would soon come by. Then the rabbit hid himself in the bushes, so that his long ears wouldn't show. For he knew that if the boys saw them, they would know right away he wasn't a tiger, no matter if he was striped like one.

In a few minutes along came the boys, and they were talking about what they were going to do to Fido, and how they would put him in a cage, and make him do lots of tricks. All of a sudden there was a rustling in the bushes, and Uncle Wiggily just stuck out his head and part of his body, laying his ears flat back where they could not be seen. But the boys could see the mud stripes, only they didn't know they were just mud, you understand.

"Oh! See that!" cried one boy.

"Yes, it's a tigery-tiger!" exclaimed the other boy.

"Let's run!" shouted both the boys together. "The tiger will eat us up!"

And just then Uncle Wiggily growled as loudly as he could, a real fierce growl, and he rattled the bushes and stuck out his striped paws, and those boys dropped Fido Flip-Flop, and ran away, as hard as they could through the woods, leaving Fido to join the rabbit.

"Thank you very much for saving me, Uncle Wiggily," said the dog, as soon as he got over being frightened. "That was a good trick, to pretend you were a tiger. But I knew you right away, only, of course, I wasn't going to tell those boys who you were. It served them right, for squeezing me the way they did. Now we'll go on, and see if we can find a fortune for you."

So they went back to where Uncle Wiggily had left his valise, and there it was safe and sound, and inside it were some nice things to eat, and the rabbit and doggie had a dinner there in the woods, after the mud stripes were washed off.

Then they went on and on, for ever so long, and nothing happened, except that a mosquito bit Fido on the end of his nose, and every time he sneezed it tickled him.

"Well, I guess we won't have anymore adventures today, Uncle Wiggily," spoke the doggie, but, a moment later, they heard a rustling in the bushes and, before they could hide themselves, out jumped Arabella Chick, the sister of Charlie, the rooster boy.

"Oh, you dear Uncle Wiggily!" she exclaimed, "you're just in time."

"What for?" asked Uncle Wiggily; "for the train?"

"No, for my party," answered Arabella. "I'm going to have one for all my friends, and I want you to come. Will you?"

"Oh, I guess so, Arabella. But you see, I have a friend with me, and —"

"Oh, he can come too," spoke Arabella, making a bow to Fido Flip-Flop. So Uncle Wiggily introduced the doggie to the chickie girl, and the chickie girl to the doggie.

Then they went on together to the party, which was held in a nice big chicken coop.

Oh, I wish you could have been there! It was just too nice for anything! Sammie and Susie Littletail were there, and they were so glad to see Uncle Wiggily again. He said he hadn't been very lucky in finding his fortune so far, but his rheumatism was not much worse, and he was going to keep on traveling. He sent his love to all the folks, and said he'd be home some time later.

Then, of course, all the other animal friends were at the party and they played games — games of all kinds, including a new one called "Please don't sit on my hat, and I won't sit on yours." It was too funny for anything, really it was.

Then, of course, there were good things to eat. Buddy Pigg passed around the ice cream, and just as he was handing a plate of it to Jennie Chipmunk it slipped — I mean the ice cream slipped — and went right into Uncle Butter's lap. But the old goat didn't care a bit. He said it reminded him of a pail of paste, and he ate the ice cream, and Nurse Jane Fuzzy-Wuzzy got Jennie some more.

Then Flip-Flop and Uncle Wiggily did some of their tricks, and everyone said they were fine, and they thought it was the best party they had ever been at.

But all of a sudden, just as they were playing the game called "Jump on the piano, and play a queer tune," there came a knock at the door.

"Who's there?" asked Arabella Chick.

"I am," answered a voice, "and I want Uncle Wiggily Longears instantly! He must come with me!" And they all looked from the window, and there stood a big dog, dressed up like a soldier, and he had a gun with him. And he wanted Uncle Wiggily to come out, and everyone was frightened, for fear he'd shoot the old gentleman rabbit.

But please don't you get alarmed. I wouldn't have that happen for worlds, and in the next story, if I catch a fish in the milk bottle, and he doesn't bite my finger, I'll tell you about Uncle Wiggily in a parade. And it will be a Decoration Day story.

Story VII

UNCLE WIGGILY IN A PARADE

*A*rabella Chick's party seemed to break up very suddenly when the guests saw that soldier-dog with the gun waiting outside the door. Buddy Pigg slipped out of a back window, and ran home with his tail behind him. Oh, excuse me, guinea pigs don't have a tail, do they? Anyhow he ran home, and so did Sammie and Susie Littletail, and Johnnie and Billie Bushytail, and the Wibblewobble children, and Peetie and Jackie Bow Wow too.

But, of course, Arabella Chick couldn't run home because she was at home already, so she just looked out of the window once more, and there the dog-soldier stood, and he was looking in his gun to see if it was loaded.

"Well, is Uncle Wiggily coming out?" called the dog again.

"I guess I am — that is — are you sure you want me?" asked the poor old gentleman rabbit, puzzled like.

"Yes, of course I want you," replied the dog.

"Then I guess I've got to go!" exclaimed Uncle Wiggily, as he looked for his crutch and valise. "I guess this is the end of my fortune-hunting. Good-bye everybody!" And he felt so badly that two big tears rolled down his ears — I mean his eyes.

Well, he bravely walked out of the door, and as he did so the dog-soldier, with the gun, exclaimed:

"Ah, here you are at last! Now hurry up, Uncle Wiggily, or we'll be late for the parade!"

And, would you believe it? that dog was good, kind, old Percival, who used to be in a circus. And of course he wouldn't hurt the rabbit gentleman for anything. Percival just put his gun to his shoulder, and said:

"Come on, we'll get in the parade now."

"Parade? What parade?" asked Uncle Wiggily. "Oh my! how you frightened me!"

"Why the Decoration Day parade," answered Percival. "Today is the day when we put flowers on the soldiers' graves, and remember them for being so brave as to go to war. All old soldiers march in the parade, and so do all their friends. I'm going to march, and I'm going to put flowers on a lot of soldiers' graves. I happened to remember that you were once in the war, so I came for you. I didn't mean to scare you. You were in the war, weren't you?"

"Yes," said Uncle Wiggily, happy now because he knew he wasn't going to get shot, "I once went to war, and killed a lot of mosquitoes."

"Good! I thought so!" exclaimed Percival. "Well, I met Grandfather Goosey Gander, and he said he thought you were at this party, so I came for you. Come on, now, the parade is almost ready to start."

"Oh, how you did frighten us!" exclaimed Arabella, whose heart was still going pitter-patter. "We thought you were going to hurt Uncle Wiggily, Percival."

"Oh, I'm so sorry I alarmed you," spoke the circus dog politely. "I won't do it again."

Well, in a little while Percival and Uncle Wiggily were at the parade. The old gentleman rabbit left his satchel at Arabella's house, and only took his crutch. But he limped along just like a real soldier, and Percival carried his gun as bravely as one could wish.

Oh, I wish you could have heard the bands playing, and the drums beating – the little kind that sound like when you drop beans on the kitchen oilcloth, and the big drums, that go "Boom-boom!" like thunder and lightning, and the fifes that squeak like a mouse in the cheese trap, and then the big blaring horns, that make a sound like a circus performance.

They were all there, and there were lots of soldiers and horses and wagons filled with flowers to put on the graves of the soldiers, who were so brave that they didn't mind going to war to fight for their country, though war is a terrible thing.

Then the march began, and Uncle Wiggily and Percival stepped out as brave as anyone in all the parade. Oh, how fine they looked! and, when they marched past, all the animal people, and some real boys and girls, and papas and mammas clapped their hands and cried "Hurrah!" at the sight of the old gentleman rabbit limping along on his crutch, with the dog-soldier marching beside him.

"Who knows," whispered Percival to Uncle Wiggily, "who knows but what you may discover your fortune today?"

"Indeed I may," answer Uncle Wiggily. "Who knows?"

Well, that was a fine parade. But something happened. I was afraid it would, but I'll tell you all about it, and you can see for yourself whether or not I was right.

All of a sudden one man, with a big horn — a horn large enough to put a loaf of mother's bread down inside the noisy end — all of a sudden this man blew a terrible blast — "Umpty-umpty-Umph! Umph!" My, what a noise he made on that horn.

Now, right in front of this man was a little boy-duck riding on a pony. Yes, you've guessed who he was — he was Jimmy Wibblewobble. And when that man blew the loud blast, the pony was frightened, and ran away with Jimmie on his back.

Faster and faster ran the pony, and Jimmie Wibblewobble clung to his back, fearing every moment he would be thrown off. In and out among the people and animals in the parade, in and out among trolley cars and automobiles, in and out, and from one side to another of the street ran the frightened pony.

"Oh, poor Jimmie will be killed!" cried Percival.

"No, he will not, for I will save him!" shouted Uncle Wiggily. So that brave rabbit ran right out to where he saw Munchie Trot, the little pony boy.

"Let me jump on your back, Munchie," said Uncle Wiggily, "and then we'll race after that runaway pony and grab off poor Jimmie. And run as fast as you can, Munchie!"

"I certainly will!" cried Munchie. So Uncle Wiggily got on Munchie's back, and away they started after the runaway pony.

Faster and faster ran Munchie, and by this time the other little horsie was getting tired. Jimmie was still clinging to his back, and asking him not to run so fast, but the pony was so frightened he didn't listen to the duck-boy.

Then, just as he was going to run into a hot peanut wagon, and maybe toss Jimmie off into the red-hot roaster, all at once Uncle Wiggily, on Munchie's back, galloped up alongside of the runaway pony. And as quick as you can drink a glass of lemonade, Uncle Wiggily grabbed Jimmie up on Munchie's back beside him, and so saved the duck-boy's life. And then the runaway pony stopped short, all of a sudden, and didn't bump into the hot peanut wagon, after all, and he was sorry he had run away, and scared folks.

Then the Decoration Day parade went on, and everyone said how brave Uncle Wiggily was. But he hadn't yet found his fortune, and so in the story after this in case our front porch doesn't run away, and take the back steps with it, so I have to sleep on the doormat, I'll tell you about Uncle Wiggily in the fountain.

Story VIII

UNCLE WIGGILY IN THE FOUNTAIN

W ell, after the Decoration Day parade, and the things that happened in it, such as the pony running away with Jimmie Wibblewobble, Uncle Wiggily Longears thought he'd like to go off to some quiet place and rest.

"Oh, can't you come with me?" asked Percival, the old circus dog. "We'll go to the Bow-Wows house, and have something to eat."

"No, I'm afraid I can't go," replied the old gentleman rabbit. "You see I must travel on to seek my fortune, for I haven't found it yet, and I still have the rheumatism."

"Why don't you try to lose that rheumatism somewhere?" asked Percival. "I would, if it's such a bother."

"Oh, I've tried and tried and tried, but I can't seem to lose it," replied Uncle Wiggily. "So I think I'll travel on. I'm much obliged to you for letting me march in the parade."

Then the old gentleman rabbit got his valise, and, with his crutch, he once more started off. He went on and on, up one hill and down another, over the fields where the horses and cows and sheep were pulling up the grass, and chewing it, so the man wouldn't have to cut it with the lawn mower; on and on he went. Then Uncle Wiggily reached the woods, where the ferns and wild flowers grow.

"This is a fine place," he said as he sat down on a flat stump. "I think I will eat my dinner," so he opened the satchel, and took out a sandwich made of yellow carrots and red beets, and very pretty they looked on the white bread, let me tell you; very nice indeed!

Uncle Wiggily was eating away, and he was brushing the crumbs off his nose by wiggling his ears, when, all of a sudden, he heard a cat crying. Oh, such a loud cry as it was!

"Why, some poor kittie must be lost," thought the old gentleman rabbit. "I'll see if I can find it."

Then the cry sounded again, and, in another moment, out of a tree flew a big bird.

"Oh, maybe that bird stuck his sharp beak in the kittie and made it cry," thought Uncle Wiggily. "Bird, did you do that?" he asked, calling to the bird, who was flying around in the air.

"Did I do what?" asked the bird.

"Did you stick the kittie, and make it cry?"

"Oh, no," answered the bird. "I made that cat-crying noise myself. I am a cat-bird, you know," and surely enough that bird went "Mew! Mew! Mew!" three times, just like that, exactly as if a cat had cried under your window, when you were trying to go to sleep.

"Ha! That is very strange!" exclaimed the rabbit. "So you are a cat-bird."

"Yes, and my little birds are kittie-birds," was the answer. "I'll show you."

So the bird went "Mew! Mew! Mew!" again, and a lot of the little birds came flying around and they all went "Mew! Mew!" too, just like kitties. Oh, I tell you cat-birds are queer things! and how they do love cherries when they are ripe! Eh?

"That is very good crying, birdies," said Uncle Wiggily, "and I think I'll give you something to eat, to pay for it." So he took out from his valise some peanuts, that Percival, the circus dog, had given him, and Uncle Wiggily fed them to the cat-bird and her kittie-birds.

"You are very kind," said the mamma bird, "and if we can ever do you a favor we will."

And now listen, as the telephone girl says, those birds are going to do Uncle Wiggily a favor in a short time — a very short time indeed.

Well, after the birds had eaten all the peanuts they flew away, and Uncle Wiggily started off once more. He hadn't gone very far before he came to a fountain. You know what that is. It's a thing in a park that squirts up water, just like when you fill a rubber ball with milk or lemonade and squeeze it. Only a fountain is bigger, of course.

This fountain that Uncle Wiggily came to had no water in it, for it was being cleaned. There was a big basin, with a pipe up through the middle, and this was where the water spouted up when it was running.

"This is very strange," said Uncle Wiggily, for he had never seen a fountain before, "perhaps I can find my fortune in here. I'll go look." So down he jumped into the big empty fountain basin, which was as large as seven wash tubs made into one. And it was so nice and comfortable there, and so shady, for there were trees near it, that, before he knew it, Uncle Wiggily fell fast asleep, with his head on his satchel for a pillow.

And then he had a funny dream. He dreamed that it was raining, and that his umbrella turned inside out, and got full of holes, and that he was getting all wet.

"My!" exclaimed Uncle Wiggily, as he gave a big sneeze. "This is a very real dream. I actually believe I *am* wet!"

Then he got real wide awake all of a sudden, and he found that he was right in the middle of a lot of wetness, for the man had turned the water on in the fountain unexpectedly, not knowing that the old gentleman rabbit was asleep there.

"I must get out of here!" cried Uncle Wiggily, as he grabbed up his valise and crutch. Then the water came up to his little short, stumpy tail. Next it rose higher, up to his knees. Then it rose still faster up to his front feet and then almost up to his chin.

"Oh, I'm afraid I'm going to drown!" he cried. "I must get out!" So he tried to swim to the edge of the fountain, but you can't swim very well with a crutch and a valise, you know, and Uncle Wiggily didn't want to lose either one. Then the water from the top of the fountain splashed in his eyes and he couldn't see which way to swim.

"Oh, help! Help!" he cried. "Will no one help me?"

"Yes, we will help you!" answered a voice, and up flew the big cat-bird, and her little kitten-birds. "Quick, children!" she cried, "we must save Uncle Wiggily, who was so kind to us! Everyone of you get a stick, and we'll make a little boat, or raft, for him!"

Well, I wish you could have seen how quickly the mamma cat-bird and her kittie-birds gathered a lot of sticks, and twigs, and laid them together crossways on the water in that fountain basin, until they had a regular little boat. Upon this Uncle Wiggily climbed, with his crutch and valise, and then the mamma cat-bird flew on ahead, and pulled the boat by a string to the edge of the fountain, where the rabbit could safely get out.

So that's how the bunny was saved from drowning in the water, and in the next story, if a big, red ant doesn't crawl upon our porch and carry away the hammock, I'll tell you another adventure Uncle Wiggily had. It will be a story of the old gentleman rabbit and the bad dog.

Story IX

UNCLE WIGGILY AND THE DOG

*U*ncle Wiggily's rheumatism was quite bad after he got wet in the fountain, as I told you in the other story, and when he thanked the mamma cat-bird and her kitten-birds for saving him, he found that he could hardly walk, much less carry his heavy valise.

"Oh, we'll help you," said Mrs. Cat-Bird. "Here, Flitter and Flutter, you carry the satchel for Uncle Wiggily, and we'll take him to our house."

"But, mamma," said Flutter, who was getting to be quite a big bird-boy, "Uncle Wiggily can't climb up a tree to our nest."

"No, but we can make him a nice warm bed on the ground," said the mamma bird. "So you and Flitter carry the satchel. Put a long blade of grass through the handle, and then each of you take hold of one end of the grass in your bills, and fly away with it. Skimmer, you and Dartie go on ahead, and get something ready to eat, and I'll show Uncle Wiggily the way."

So Flitter and Flutter, the two boy birds, flew away with the satchel, and Skimmer and Dartie, the girl birds, flew on ahead to set the table, and put on the teakettle on the stove to boil, and Mrs. Cat-Bird flew slowly on over Uncle Wiggily, to show him the way.

Well, pretty soon, not so so very long, they came to where the birds lived. And those good children had already started to make a nest on the ground for the old gentleman rabbit. They had it almost finished, and by the time supper was ready it was all done. Then came the meal, and those birds couldn't do enough for Uncle Wiggily, because they liked him so.

When it got dark, they covered him all up, with soft leaves in the nest on the ground, and there he slept until morning. His rheumatism wasn't quite so bad when, after breakfast, he had sat out in the warm sun for a while, and after a bit he said:

"Well, I think I'll travel along now, and see if I can find my fortune today. Perhaps I may, and if I do I'll come back and bring you more peanuts."

"Oh, that'll be fine and dandy!" cried Flitter and Flutter, and Skimmer and Dartie. So they said good-bye to the old gentleman rabbit, and once more he started off.

"My! I'm certainly getting to be a great traveler," he thought as he walked along through the woods and over the fields. "But I don't ever seem to get to anyplace. Something always happens to me. I hope everything goes along nicely today."

But you just wait and see what takes place. I'm afraid something is going to happen very shortly, but it's not my fault, and all I can do is to tell you exactly all about it. Wait! There, it's beginning to happen now.

All of a sudden, as Uncle Wiggily was traveling along, he came to a place in the woods where a whole lot of Gypsies had their wagons and tents. And on one tent, in which was an old brown and wrinkled Gypsy lady, there was a sign which read:

FORTUNES TOLD HERE.

"Ha! If they tell fortunes in that tent, perhaps the Gypsy lady can tell me where to find mine," thought Uncle Wiggily. "I'll go up and ask her."

Well, he was just going to the tent when he happened to think that perhaps the Gypsy woman wouldn't understand rabbit talk. So he sat there in the bushes thinking what he had better do, when all at once, before he could wiggle his ears more than four times, a great big, bad, ugly dog sprang at him, barking, oh! so loudly.

"Come on, Browser!" cried this dog to another one. "Here is a fat rabbit that we can catch for dinner. Come on, let's chase him!"

Well, you can just imagine how frightened Uncle Wiggily was. He didn't sit there, waiting for that dog to catch him, either. No, indeed, and a bag of popcorn besides! Up jumped Uncle Wiggily, with his crutch and his valise, and he hopped as hard and as fast as he could run. My! How his legs did twist in and out.

"Come on! Come!" barked the first dog to the second one.

"I'm coming! I'm coming! Woof! Woof! Bow-w-w Bow-wow!" barked the second dog.

Poor Uncle Wiggily's heart beat faster and faster, and he didn't know which way to run. Every way he turned the dogs were after him, and soon more of the savage animals came to join the first two, until all the dogs in that Gypsy camp were chasing the poor old gentleman rabbit.

"I guess I'll have to drop my satchel or my crutch," thought Uncle Wiggily. "I can't carry them much farther. Still, I don't want to lose them." So he held on to them a little longer, took a good breath and ran on some more.

He thought he saw a chance to escape by running across in front of the fortune-telling tent, and he started that way, but a Gypsy man, with a gun, saw him and fired at him. I'm glad to say, however, that he didn't shoot Uncle Wiggily, or else I couldn't tell anymore stories about him.

Uncle Wiggily got safely past the tent, but the dogs were almost up to him now. One of them was just going to catch him by his left hind leg, when one of the Gypsy men cried out:

"Grab him, Biter! Grab him! We'll have rabbit potpie for dinner; that's what we'll have!"

Wasn't that a perfectly dreadful way to talk about our Uncle Wiggily? But just wait, if you please.

Biter, the bad dog, was just going to grab the rabbit, when all of a sudden, Uncle Wiggily saw a big hole in the ground.

"That's what I'm looking for!" he exclaimed. "I'm going down there, and hide away from these dogs!"

So into the hole he popped, valise, crutch and all, and oh! how glad he was to get into the cool, quiet darkness, leaving those savage, barking dogs outside. But wait a moment longer, if you please.

Biter and Browser stopped short at the hole.

"He's gone – gotten clean away!" exclaimed Browser. "Isn't that too bad?"

"No, we'll get him yet!" cried Biter. "Here, you watch at this hole, while I go get a pail of water. We'll pour the water down, under the ground where the rabbit is, and that will make him come out, and we'll eat him."

"Good!" cried Browser. So while he stood there and watched, Biter went for the water. But, mind you, Uncle Wiggily had sharp ears and he heard what they were saying, and what do you think he did?

Why, with his sharp claws he went right to work, and he dug, and dug, and dug in the back part of that underground place, until he had made another hole, far off from the first one, and he crawled out of that, with his crutch and valise, just as Biter was pouring the water down the first hole.

"Ah, ha! I think this will astonish those dogs!" thought Uncle Wiggily, and he took a peep at them from behind a bush where they couldn't see him, and then he hopped on through the woods, to look for more adventures, leaving the dogs still pouring water.

And one happened to him shortly after that, as I shall tell you on the next page, when, in case the rocking chair doesn't tip over backwards and spill out the sofa cushion into the rubber plant, the story will be about Uncle Wiggily and the monkey.

Story X

UNCLE WIGGILY AND THE MONKEY

*L*et me see, we left those two bad dogs pouring water down the hole, to get Uncle Wiggily out, didn't we? And the old gentleman rabbit fooled them, didn't he? He got out of another hole that he dug around by the back door, you remember.

Well, I just wish you could have seen those two dogs, after they had poured pail after pail of water down the hole, and no rabbit came floating up.

"This hole must go all the way down to China!" said Browser, breathing very fast.

"Yes, I'm tired of carrying water," said Biter. And just then another dog cried out:

"Why, foolish dogs, the water's all running out the back way!" And, surely enough, it was. Then they knew Uncle Wiggily had escaped, and they were as angry as anything, but it served them right, I think.

"My! I wonder what will happen next?" thought the old gentleman rabbit, as he hopped along. "That was a narrow escape."

So, having nothing else to do, Uncle Wiggily sat down on a nice, smooth stump, and he ate some lunch out of his valise. And a red ant came up, and very politely asked if she might not pick up the crumbs which the old rabbit dropped.

"Of course you may," said Uncle Wiggily kindly. "And I'll give you a whole slice of bread and butter, also."

"Oh, you are too generous," spoke the red ant. "I never could carry a slice of bread and butter. But if you will leave it on the stump I'll get some of my friends, and we'll bite off little crumbs, a few at a time, and in that way carry it to our houses."

So that's what Uncle Wiggily did, and the ants had a fine feast, and they were very thankful. Uncle Wiggily asked them if they knew where he could find his fortune.

"Why don't you go to work, instead of traveling around so much?" asked the biggest red ant. "The best fortune is the one you work for."

"Is it? I never thought of that," said Uncle Wiggily. "I will look for work at once. I wonder if you ants have any for me."

"We'd like to help you," they said, "but you see you are so large that you couldn't get into our houses to do any work. You had much better travel along, and work for someone larger than we are."

"I will," decided the old gentleman rabbit. "I'll ask everyone I meet if they want me to work for them."

So he started off once more, and the first place he came to was a house where a mouse lady lived.

"Have you any work I can do?" asked Uncle Wiggily politely.

"What work can you do?" asked the mouse lady.

"Well, I can peel carrots or turnips with my teeth," said Uncle Wiggily, "and I can look after children, and tell them stories, and I can do some funny tricks —"

"Then you had better go join a circus," interrupted the mouse lady. "I have no children, and I can peel my own carrots, thank you. As for turnips, I never eat them."

"Then I must go on a little further," said Uncle Wiggily, as he picked up his valise, and walked off on his crutch. So he went on, until he came to another house in the woods, and he knocked on the door.

"Have you any work I can do?" inquired Uncle Wiggily politely.

"No! Get away and don't bother me!" growled a most unpleasant voice, and the rabbit was just going down the steps, when the door opened a crack, and a long, sharp nose and a mouth full of sharp teeth, and some long legs with sharp claws on them, were stuck out.

"Oh, hold on!" cried the voice. "I guess I can find some work for you after all. You can get up a dinner for me!" and then the savage creature, who had opened the door, made a grab for the rabbit and nearly caught him. Only Uncle Wiggily jumped away, just in time, and the wolf, for he it was who had called out, caught his own tail in the crack of the door and howled most frightfully.

"Come back! Come back!" cried the wolf, but, of course, Uncle Wiggily wouldn't do such a foolish thing as that, and the wolf couldn't chase after him, for his tail was fast in the door hinge.

"My, I must be more careful after this how I knock at doors, and ask for work," the old gentleman rabbit thought. "I was nearly caught that time. I'll try again, and I may have better luck."

So he walked along through the woods, and pretty soon he heard a voice singing, and this is the song, as nearly as I can remember it:

Here I sit and wonder
What I'm going to do.
I've no one to help me,
I think it's sad; don't you?

I have to play the fiddle,
But still I'd give a cent
To anyone who'd keep the boys
From crawling in the tent.

"Well, I wonder who that can be?" thought Uncle Wiggily. "He'll give a cent, eh? to anyone who keeps the boys from crawling in the tent. Now, if that isn't a bear or a fox or a wolf maybe I can work for him, and earn that money. I'll try."

So he peeped out of the bushes, and there he saw a nice monkey, all dressed up in a clown's suit, spotted red, white and blue. And the monkey was playing a tune on a fiddle. Then, all of a sudden, he laid aside the fiddle, and began to beat the bass drum. Then he blew on a horn, next he jumped up and down, and turned a somersault, and then, finally, he grabbed up a whip with a whistle in the tail — I mean in the end — and that monkey began to pretend he was chasing make-believe boys from around a real tent that was in a little place under the trees.

"Oh, I guess that monkey won't hurt me," said Uncle Wiggily as he stepped boldly out, and as soon as the monkey saw the rabbit, he called most politely:

"Well, what do you want?"

"I want to earn a cent, by chasing boys from out the tent," replied Uncle Wiggily.

"Good!" cried the monkey. "So you heard me sing? I'm tired of being the whole show. I need someone to help me. Come over here and I'll explain all about it. If you like it, you can go to work for me, and if you do, your fortune is as good as made."

"That's fine!" cried Uncle Wiggily. "And I can do tricks in the show, too."

"Fine!" exclaimed the monkey, hanging by his tail from a green apple tree. "Now, I'll explain."

But, just as he was going to do so, out jumped a big black bear from the bushes, making a grab for Uncle Wiggily. He might have caught him, too, only the monkey picked up a coconut pie off the ground and hit the bear so hard on the head, that the savage creature was frightened, and ran away, sneezing, leaving the monkey and the rabbit alone by the show-tent.

"Now, we'll get ready to have some fun," said the monkey, and what he and Uncle Wiggily did I'll tell you in the following story which will be about the old gentleman rabbit and the boys — that is, if the molasses jug doesn't tip over on my plate, and spoil my bread and butter peanut sandwich.

Story XI

UNCLE WIGGILY AND THE BOYS

"*W*ell," said the monkey after the bear had run away. "I guess we can now sit down and talk quietly together; eh, Uncle Wiggily?"

"Yes," said the old gentleman rabbit. "But what is it that you want me to do? I heard you sing that funny little song, about the boys coming in the tent. But I don't exactly understand."

"That's just it," replied the monkey. "You see, it's this way. I have a little sort of a circus-show here, and the troublesome boys don't want to pay any money to get in. So when my back is turned they crawl under the tent, and so they see the show for nothing — just like at the circus."

"Oh, so that's how it is?" asked Uncle Wiggily. "And you want me to keep out the boys?"

"That's it," said the monkey. "Here's a big stick, with which to tickle the boys who crawl in under the tent without paying. Now I'll practice my tricks."

So the monkey did a lot of tricks. He stood on his head, and he hung by his tail, and he danced around in a circle. Then he pounded the drum, not so hard as to hurt it, but hard enough to make a noise, and he played the fiddle and blew on the horn, and then he ran inside the tent and jumped over a bench, making believe it was an elephant, and he did all sorts of funny tricks like that. He even stood on his head, and made a funny face.

"That will make a very nice show," said Uncle Wiggily after he had watched the monkey. "Now I'll stay outside, and keep the boys from coming in unless they pay their money. And you can be inside, doing the tricks."

"And I'll give you money for working for me," said the monkey. "Then perhaps you can make your fortune, and, besides that, I'll give you a coconut, and you can make a coconut pie with it."

"That will be fine!" cried Uncle Wiggily. So he and the monkey practiced to get ready for their show. It was a nice little tent in which it was to be given, and there were seats for the people, who would come, and a platform, and flying rings and trapeze bars and paper hoops, and all things like that, just the same as in a real circus. Well, finally the time came for the show. It was the day after Uncle Wiggily got to the place where the tent was, and he had slept that night in a hammock, put up between two trees.

"Now we're almost ready for the show," said the monkey to the old gentleman rabbit, after a bit, "so I hope you will be sure to keep out the troublesome boys. They always creep under the tent, and see the show for nothing. I can't have that going on if I'm to make any money."

"Oh, I'll stop 'em!" declared Uncle Wiggily.

"And here's the club to do it with," said the monkey, handing Uncle Wiggily a stick.

"Oh, I don't know about that," answered the rabbit. "I never hurt boys if I can help it. Perhaps I shan't need the club. I'll leave it here."

So Uncle Wiggily hid the club under an apple tree, but the monkey said it would be needed, and he wanted Uncle Wiggily to keep it, and take a whip, too. But the old rabbit shook his head.

"I'll try being kind to the boys," he said. "You let me have my way, Mr. Monkey."

Well, pretty soon, not so very long, the show began. The monkey went inside the tent, and he blew on the horn, and he made music on the fiddle, and sang a funny song about a little great big pussy, who had a red balloon. She stuck a pin inside it, and it played a go-bang! tune.

Of course, as soon as the show started the people came crowding up to the tent, just as they do at the circus. There were men and women, and little boys and girls, and big boys and girls, and they all wanted to get inside to see what the monkey was doing. But, do you know, I believe all that he was doing was playing monkey-doodle tricks — but, of course, I might be mistaken.

Well, as it always happens, some boys didn't have any money with which to pay their way inside the tent. And, of course, as it will sometimes happen, one boy said to another:

"Hey! I know a way we can crawl in under the tent, and see the show, and not have anything to pay."

"But that wouldn't be fair," spoke the other boy. "It would be cheating, and there's nothing meaner in this world than to cheat, whether it's playing a baseball game or going to a circus."

"I guess you're right," said the first boy. "What shall we do, though? I want to see the show."

"Well, we must be fair, anyhow," spoke the second boy. "We can't crawl in under the tent, but perhaps if we ask the monkey to let us in for nothing he'll do it."

"Very well, we will," said the first boy. So they went up to the monkey and asked if they could go in for nothing, but, of course, he wouldn't let them.

"May we crawl in under the tent, then?" asked the second boy.

"If Uncle Wiggily will let you," answered the monkey, blinking his two eyes and wrapping his tail around his neck.

So those boys tried to crawl in under the tent, and as soon as Uncle Wiggily saw them he rushed up and cried out:

"Hey! Hold on there! Nobody must go under the tent. You must buy a ticket," and he shook a feather at the boys and, instead of hitting them, he only tickled them, and didn't hurt them a bit, for they sneezed.

Well, those boys were very troublesome. They kept on trying to crawl under the tent, and Uncle Wiggily rushed here, there and around the corner trying to stop them, and he cracked the lash on his whip, just like the man in the circus ring. But those boys kept on trying to crawl under the tent, for the monkey had given them permission, you see.

So finally Uncle Wiggily said:

"I'll give those boys a little show myself, outside the tent, for nothing. Then maybe they'll stop bothering me."

So he stood on his left ear, and then on his right ear, and then he jumped through a hoop, and rolled over, and barked liked a dog, and all the boys that had tried to crawl under the tent to see the monkey-show for nothing, ran out to see Uncle Wiggily's show.

And he did lots of tricks and kept them all from crawling in under the tent, and he even ate a popcorn ball, standing on his hind legs, and wiggling his left ear with a pin-wheel on it. Then, after a while, the monkey-show was all over, and the monkey said:

"Uncle Wiggily, you did very well. You treated those troublesome boys just fine! So I'll give you ten pennies, and perhaps they will make you have a good fortune."

Then the monkey gave Uncle Wiggily ten pennies, and he went to sleep in a feather bed, while the old gentleman rabbit went down to the drug store to get an ice cream soda.

And what happened after the show was over, and what Uncle Wiggily did after he had his ice cream, I'll tell you in the next story which will be about Uncle Wiggily in a balloon. That is, if our pussy cat doesn't get all covered with red paint, and look like a tomato growing on a strawberry vine. So watch out, and don't let that happen.

Story XII

UNCLE WIGGILY IN A BALLOON

*W*ell, just as I expected, something happened to my pussy-cat named Peter. He didn't fall into the pot of red paint, but he either ran away, or else someone took him. So now I have no pussy-cat. But I'll tell you a story about Uncle Wiggily just the same.

The old gentleman rabbit stayed with the monkey for several days, and he was so kind and good to the troublesome boys – Uncle Wiggily was, I mean – and he did such funny tricks for them, that they didn't crawl under the tent anymore, and the monkey could do his tricks in peace and quietness.

"Oh, you have been a great help to me," said the monkey to the rabbit, "and I would like you to work for me all Summer. I am now going to travel on to the next town, and if you like you may go with me and keep the boys there from crawling under the tent."

"No, I thank you," replied Uncle Wiggily slowly, as he put some bread and butter, and a piece of pie, into his satchel. "I think I will travel farther on by myself, and seek my fortune."

"Well, I'm sorry to see you go," said the monkey. "And here is fifty cents for your work. I hope you have good luck."

And then Uncle Wiggily started off again, over the fields and through the woods, seeking his fortune, while the monkey got ready to move his show to the next town.

Well, for some time nothing happened to the old gentleman rabbit. He walked on and on, and once he saw a little red ant, trying to drag a piece of cake home for dinner. The cake was so big that the ant was having a dreadful time with it, but Uncle Wiggily took his left ear, and just brushed that cake into the ant's house as easily as anything.

"My, how strong and brave you are," cried the little red ant. "Won't you let me get you a glass of water?"

"I would like it," said the rabbit, "for it is quite warm today."

Well, that ant got Uncle Wiggily a glass of water, but you know how it is — an ant's glass is so very small that it only holds as much water as you could put on the point of a pin, and really, I'm not exaggerating a bit, when I say that Uncle Wiggily drank seventeen thousand four hundred and twenty-six and a half ant-glasses of water before he had enough. It took all the ants for a mile around to bring the water to him, but they didn't mind, because they liked him.

Then the old gentleman rabbit traveled on again, and when it came night he slept under a haystack.

"I am sure I'll find my fortune today," thought Uncle Wiggily as he got up and brushed the hay seed out of his ears the next morning.

It was a bright, beautiful day, and he hadn't gone very far before he heard some fine music.

"My, there must be a hand-organ around here," he said to himself. "And perhaps there is another monkey. I'll watch out."

So he stood on his hind legs, Uncle Wiggily did, and the music played louder, and all of a sudden the rabbit looked down the road, and there was a nice circus, with the white tents, all covered with flags, and bands playing, and elephants squirting water through their long noses over their backs to wash the dust off. And lions and tigers were roaring, and the horses were running, and the fat lady was drinking pink lemonade, and Oh! it was fine!

"I've got fifty cents, and I guess I'll go to the circus," thought Uncle Wiggily, and he was just entering the big tent when he happened to see a man with a lot of red and green and yellow and pink balloons. Now, you would have thought that man would have been happy, having so many balloons, but he wasn't. He looked very sad, that man did, and he was almost crying.

"Poor man!" thought Uncle Wiggily. "Perhaps he has no money to go in the circus. I'll give him mine. Here is fifty cents, Mr. Man," said the old gentleman rabbit, kindly. "Take it and go see the elephant eat peanuts."

"Oh, that is very good of you," spoke the balloon man, "but I don't want to go to the circus. I want to sell my balloons, but no one will buy them."

"Why not?" asked the rabbit.

"Oh, because there are so many other things to buy," said the man, "red peanuts and lemonade in shells — oh, I've got that wrong, it is red lemonade, isn't it? And peanuts in shells. But no matter. What I need," said the man, "is to get the people to listen to me — I need to make them look at me, and when they see what fine balloons I have they'll buy some. But there are so many other things to look at that they never look toward me at all."

"Ha! I know the very thing!" cried Uncle Wiggily. "You ought to have someone go up in a balloon. That would surprise the people like anything. They'd be sure to look at that, and they'd all run over here and buy all your balloons."

"Yes, but who can I get to go up in a balloon?" asked the man.

"I will!" cried Uncle Wiggily bravely. "Perhaps I may find my fortune up in the sky, so I'll go in a balloon."

Well, the man thought that was fine. So he made a little basket for the rabbit to sit in, and he fastened the basket to a big red balloon, and then he took care of the rabbit's valise for him, while Uncle Wiggily got ready to go toward the clouds, taking only his crutch with him.

When the man had everything fixed and when the rabbit was sitting in the basket as easily as in a soft chair at home, the man cried:

"Over here! Over here, everybody! Over here, people! A rabbit is going up in a balloon! A most wonderful sight! Over here!"

And then the man let go of the balloon, and Uncle Wiggily shot right up toward the sky, only, of course, the man had a string fast to the balloon to pull it down again. Up and up went the balloon carrying Uncle Wiggily. Up and up!

And my! how surprised the people were. They rushed over and bought so many balloons that the man couldn't take in the money fast enough. And Uncle Wiggily stayed up there, high in the air, looking for his fortune.

And then, all of a sudden, a bad boy, with a bean shooter, shot at the balloon, and "bang!" it burst, with a big hole in it. Down came Uncle Wiggily, head over heels, bursted balloon, basket, crutch and all.

"Oh, he'll be killed! He'll be killed!" cried all the people.

"No, he'll not! We'll save him!" cried Dickie and Nellie Chip-Chip, the boy and girl sparrow, who happened to be at the circus. "We'll save Uncle Wiggily!"

So up into the air they flew, and before Uncle Wiggily could fall to the ground Dickie and Nellie grabbed the basket in their bills, and, by fluttering their wings, they let it come very gently to earth just like a feather falling, and the rabbit wasn't hurt a bit. But, of course, the balloon was broken.

So that's how Uncle Wiggily went up in a balloon and came down again, but he hadn't yet found his fortune. And now in the next story, if our fire shovel doesn't go out to play in the sand pile, and get its ears full of dirt, I'll tell you about Uncle Wiggily in an automobile.

Story XIII

UNCLE WIGGILY IN AN AUTO

*W*ell, after Uncle Wiggily had been saved from the falling balloon by Dickie and Nellie Chip-Chip, the sparrow children, the people were so excited that they wanted the bad boy arrested for making a hole in the balloon with his bean-shooter.

"No, let him go," said the rabbit gentleman, kindly. "I'm sure he won't do it again." And do you know, that boy never did. It was a good lesson to him.

Then the people bought all the balloons, until the man had none left, and I guess if he could have sent for forty-'leven more he would have sold them also.

"I will pay you good wages to stay with me, and go up in a balloon every day," said the man to the rabbit. "You would help me do lots of business."

"No," said Uncle Wiggily. "I must travel on and seek my fortune. I didn't find it up in the air."

But before the old gentleman rabbit traveled on, he went into the circus with Dickie and Nellie. For they had an extra ticket that Bully the frog was going to use, only Bully went in swimming and caught cold, and had to stay home. So Uncle Wiggily enjoyed the show very much in his place.

"Give my love to Sammie and Susie Littletail and to all my friends," said the rabbit, as he took his crutch and valise, after the circus was over, and started to travel on, looking for his fortune.

Well, the first place he came to that day was an old hollow stump, and on the door was a card which read:

COME IN

"Ha! Come in; eh?" said Uncle Wiggily. "I guess not much! You can't fool me again. There is a bad bear, or a savage owl inside that stump, and they want to eat me. I'll just stay outside."

He was just hurrying past, when the door of the stump-house opened, and an old grandfather fox stuck out his head. This fox was almost blind, and he had no teeth, and he had no claws, and his tail was just like a last year's dusting brush, that the moths have eaten most up, and altogether that fox was so old and feeble that he couldn't have hurt a mosquito. So Uncle Wiggily wasn't a bit afraid of him.

"I say, is there anything good to eat out there?" asked the fox, looking over the tops of his spectacles at the rabbit. "Anything nice and juicy to eat?"

"Yes, I am good to eat," said Uncle Wiggily, "but you are not going to eat me. Good-bye!"

"Hold on!" cried the old fox, "don't be afraid. I can only eat soup, for I have no teeth to chew with, so unless you are soup you are of no use to me."

"Well, I'm not soup, but I know how to make some," replied the rabbit, for he felt sorry for the grandfather fox.

So what do you think our Uncle Wiggily did? Why, he went into the fox's stump-house and made a big pot full of the finest kind of soup, and the rabbit and the fox ate it all up, and, because the fox had no teeth or claws, he couldn't hurt his visitor.

"I wish you would stay with me forever," said the old fox, as he blinked his eyes at Uncle Wiggily. "I have a young and strong grandson coming home soon, and you might show him how to make soup."

"No, thank you," replied the rabbit. "I'm afraid that young and strong grandson of yours would want to eat me instead of the soup, I guess I'll travel on." So the old gentleman rabbit took his crutch and valise and traveled on.

Well, pretty soon, it began to get dark, and Uncle Wiggily knew night was coming on. And he wondered where he could stay, for he didn't see any haystacks to sleep under. He was thinking that he'd have to dig a burrow in the ground for himself, and he was looking for a soft place to begin, when, all at once, he heard a loud "Honk-Honk!" back of him in the road.

"Ha, an automobile is coming!" said Uncle Wiggily. "I must get out of the way!" So he hopped on ahead, going down the road quite fast, until he got to a place where there were prickly briar bushes on both sides of the highway.

"My! I'll have to keep in the middle of the road if I don't want to get scratched," said the rabbit. And then the automobile horn behind him honked louder than ever.

"They are certainly coming along fast," thought Uncle Wiggily. "If I don't look out I'll be run over." So he hopped along quicker than before, until, all of a sudden, as he looked down the road, he saw a savage dog standing there.

"Well, now! Isn't that just my bad luck!" cried Uncle Wiggily. "If I go on the dog will catch me, and if I stand here the auto will run on top of me. I just guess I'll run back and see if there is a hole where I can crawl through the bushes."

So he started to run back, but, no sooner had he done so, than the dog saw him, and came rushing at him with a loud, "Bow-wow-wow! Bow-wow-wow!"

"My, but he's savage!" thought the rabbit. "I wonder if I can get away in time?"

And then the auto honked louder than before, and all of a sudden it came whizzing down the road, right toward the rabbit.

"Oh, dear; I'm going to be caught, sure!" cried Uncle Wiggily, and indeed it did look so, for there was the dog running from one direction, and the auto coming in the other, and prickly briar bushes were on both sides of the road, and Uncle Wiggily couldn't crawl through them without pulling all the fur off his back, and his ears, too.

"Honk-Honk!" went the auto.

"Bow-wow!" went the dog.

"Oh, dear!" cried Uncle Wiggily. Then he thought of a plan. "I'll give a big run and a long jump and maybe I can jump over the auto, and then the auto will bump into the dog, and I will be safe!" he cried.

So he took a long run, and just as the auto was going to hit him, Uncle Wiggily gave a big jump, right up into the air. He didn't jump quite quickly enough, however, for one of the big rubber tires ran over his toe, but he wasn't much hurt. And what do you think he did? Why, he landed right in the auto, on the seat beside a little boy.

And that dog was so frightened of the automobile that he howled and yowled, and his teeth chattered, and he tucked his tail between his legs, and ran home.

"Oh, the bunny! The bunny!" cried the little boy, as he saw Uncle Wiggly. "May we keep him, papa?"

"I guess so," said the boy's papa. "Anyhow his foot is hurt, and we'll take care of him until it gets well. My, but he is a good jumper, though!"

So the man stopped the auto, and picked up Uncle Wiggily's crutch and valise, which the old gentleman rabbit had dropped when he jumped upon the seat beside the boy, and then the car went on. And Uncle Wiggily wasn't a bit frightened at being in an auto, for he knew the boy and man would be kind to him.

"Perhaps I shall find my fortune now," the rabbit gentleman said. And the little boy patted him on the back, and stroked his long ears.

Now, in the story after this I'll tell you what happened to Uncle Wiggily at the little boy's house, and in case our door key doesn't get locked out, and have to sleep in the park, you are going to hear about Uncle Wiggily in a boat.

Story XIV

UNCLE WIGGILY IN A BOAT

"*P*oor rabbit!" exclaimed the little boy in the automobile, as he rubbed Uncle Wiggily's ears. "I wonder if his foot is much hurt, papa?"

"I don't know," answered the man, as he steered the machine down the road. "I'll have the doctor look at it."

"Oh, indeed, it isn't hurt much," spoke up Uncle Wiggily. "The rubber tire was soft, you see. But my rheumatism is much worse on account of running so fast."

"What's this? Well, of all things! This rabbit can talk!" cried the man in surprise.

"Of course he can, papa," said the boy. "Lots of rabbits can talk. Why, there's Sammie and Susie Littletail; they can talk, and maybe this rabbit knows them."

"I'm their uncle," said the old gentleman rabbit, making a bow.

"Oh, then, you must be Uncle Wiggily Longears!" cried the little boy. "Oh, I've always wanted to see you, and now I can!"

"Well, it is very strange to meet you this way," said the man. "Still, I am glad you are not hurt, Uncle Wiggily. And so you are out seeking your fortune," for the rabbit had told them about his travels. "Perhaps you would like to rest at our house for a few days. We can give you a nice room, with a brass bed, and a bath-tub to yourself, and you can have your meals in bed, if you can't come down stairs."

"Oh, I am not used to that kind of a life," said the old gentleman rabbit. "I would rather live out of doors. If you can get me some clean straw to lie on, and once in a while a carrot or a turnip, and a bit of lettuce and some cabbage leaves now and then, I'll be all right. And as soon as my foot is well I'll travel on."

"Oh, what good times we'll have!" cried the little boy. "Our house is near a lake, and I have a motor boat. And I'll give you a ride in it."

Well, Uncle Wiggily thought that would be nice, and he was rather glad, after all, that he had jumped into the auto. So pretty soon they came to the place where the boy lived. Oh, it was a fine, large house, with lots of grounds, lawns and gardens all around it. And there were several dogs on the place, but the little boy spoke to them all, telling them that the rabbit was his friend Uncle Wiggily, who must not be bitten or barked at on any account.

"Oh, we heard about him from Fido Flip-Flop," said big dog Rover. "We wouldn't hurt Uncle Wiggily for two worlds, and part of another one, and a bag of peanuts."

So Uncle Wiggily was given a nice bed of straw in one of the empty dog-houses, and the boy got him some cabbage and lettuce, and the rabbit made himself a sandwich of them, with some bread and butter which he had in his satchel.

Then the rabbit and the dogs talked together, and the rabbit told of his travels, and what had happened to him so far.

"Wonderful! Wonderful!" exclaimed the old dog Rover. "You should write a book about your fortune."

"I haven't found it yet, but perhaps I may, and then I'll write the book," said Uncle Wiggily, combing out his whiskers.

That night the boy put a soft rag and some salve on the rabbit's sore foot, and he also gave him some liniment for his rheumatism, and in the morning Uncle Wiggily was much better. He and the boy and the dogs had lots of fun playing together on the smooth, green, grassy lawn. They played tag, and hide-and-go-seek, and a new game called "Don't Let the Ragman Take Your Rubber Boots." And the dog Rover pretended he was the ragman.

"Now, then, we'll all go out in my motor boat," said the boy, so he and Uncle Wiggily and the dogs went down to the lake and, surely enough, there was the boat, the nicest one you could wish for. There was a little cabin in it, and seats out on deck, and a little engine that went "choo-choo!" and pushed the boat through the water.

In the boat they all had a fine ride around the lake, which was almost like the one where you go to a Sunday-school picnic, and then it was time for dinner. And, as a special treat, when they got on shore, Uncle Wiggily was given carrot ice cream, with chopped-up turnips in it. And oh, how good it was to him!

Well, the days passed, and Uncle Wiggily was getting so he could walk along pretty well, for his foot was all cured, and he began to think of going on once more to seek his fortune. And then something happened. One day the boy went out alone in a rowboat to see if he could find any fish. And before he knew it his boat had tipped over, spilling him out into the water, and he couldn't swim. Wasn't that dreadful?

"Oh! Help! Help!" he cried, as the water came up to his chin.

My, but it's awful to be tipped over in a boat! and I and I hope if you can't swim you'll never go out in one alone. And there was that poor boy splashing around in the water, and almost drowned.

"Save me! Save me!" the boy cried. "Oh, save me!"

Well, as it happened, Uncle Wiggily was walking along the shore of the lake just then. He saw the little boy fall out of the boat, and he heard him cry.

"I'll save you if I can!" exclaimed the brave old rabbit. "Come on, Rover, we'll go out in the motor boat and rescue him."

"Bow-wow! Bow-wow! Sure! Sure!" cried Cover, wagging his tail.

So he and Uncle Wiggily ran down, and jumped into the motor boat. And they knew just how to start the engine and run it, for the boy had showed them.

"Bang-bang!" went the engine. "Whizz-whizz!" went the boat through the water.

"Faster! Faster!" cried Uncle Wiggily, who was steering the boat, while Rover ran the engine. "Go faster!"

So Rover made it go as fast as he could, and then all of a sudden that boy went down under the water, out of sight.

"Oh, he's drowned!" cried Uncle Wiggily sorrowfully.

But he wasn't, I'm glad to say. Just then along came Nurse Jane Fuzzy-Wuzzy, the muskrat, swimming. And she dived away down under and helped bring that boy up to the top of the water, and then Uncle Wiggily and Cover grabbed him as the muskrat lifted him up, and they pulled him into the motor boat, and so saved his life. And oh! how thankful he was when he was safe on shore, and he was careful never to fall in the water again.

Now, in case the clothes wringer doesn't squeeze all the juice out of my breakfast orange, I'll tell you in the next story about Uncle Wiggily making a cherry pie.

Story XV

UNCLE WIGGILY MAKES A PIE

*D*o you remember the little boy whom Uncle Wiggily helped save after he fell out of the boat? Well, that boy's papa was so glad because Uncle Wiggily had helped save the little chap from drowning that he couldn't do enough for the old gentleman rabbit.

"You can stay here forever, and have carrot ice cream every day if you like," the man said.

"Oh, thank you very much, but I think I'll travel on," replied Uncle Wiggily. "I have still to seek my fortune."

"Why, *I* will give you a fortune!" said the boy's papa. "I will give you a thousand million dollars, and a penny besides."

"That would be a fine fortune," spoke the rabbit, "but I would much rather find my own. It is no fun when you get a thing given to you. It is better to earn it yourself, and then you think more of it."

"Yes, that is so," said the man. "Well, we will be sorry to see you go."

Uncle Wiggily started off the next day, once more to seek his fortune, and the little boy felt so sad at seeing him go that he cried, and put his arms around the old gentleman rabbit, and kissed him between the ears. And Uncle Wiggily felt badly, too.

Well, the old gentleman rabbit traveled on and on for several days after that, sleeping under hay stacks part of the time, or in empty hollow stumps, and sometimes he dug a burrow for himself in the soft ground.

And one afternoon, just as the sun was getting ready to go to bed for the night, Uncle Wiggily came to an open place in the woods where there was a cave, made of a lot of little stones piled up together.

"My! I wonder who lives there?" thought the rabbit. "It is too small for a giant to live in, but there may be a bad bear or a savage fox in there. I guess I'd better get away from here."

Well, Uncle Wiggily was just going, when, all at once, a voice cried out:

"Here, hold on there!"

The rabbit looked back, and he saw a great big porcupine, or hedge-hog — you know, those animals like a big grey rabbit, only their fur is the stickery-prickery kind, like needles, and the quills come out and stick in anybody who bites a hedgehog. So I hope none of you ever bite one. And they won't bite you if you don't bother them.

So as soon as Uncle Wiggily saw that it was Mr. Hedgehog who was speaking he wasn't a bit afraid, for he knew him.

"Oh, it's you, is it?" asked the rabbit. "I'm real glad to see you. I was going to travel on, but —"

"Don't say another word!" cried the hedgehog heartily. "You can stay in my cave all night. I have two beds, and it's a good thing I have, for if you slept with me you might get full of my stickery-stickers."

"Yes, I guess I had better sleep alone," said Uncle Wiggily, with a laugh. "But it seems to me, Mr. Hedgehog, that you are not looking well."

"I'm not," answered the porcupine, as he shivered so that several of his quills fell out on the grass. "I'm suffering for some cherry pie. Oh, cherry pie! If I only had some I know I'd feel better at once. I just love it!"

"Why don't you make some yourself?" asked Uncle Wiggily.

"I have tried," replied the hedgehog. "I've tried and tried again, but, somehow, it never comes out right. Here, I'll show you. I made a cherry pie just before I looked out of the door and saw you. I'll show it to you."

He went into his little stone house, and Uncle Wiggily went with him.

"There's the pie — it's no good!" cried the porcupine, as he pointed to something on the table. Well, as soon as Uncle Wiggily saw it he laughed so hard that his ears waved back and forth.

"What's the matter? I don't see anything funny," asked Mr. Hedge-hog, shivering so that more quills fell out.

"Why, you've gone and put the cherry pits into the pie instead of the cherries," said the rabbit. "That's no way to do. You must take out the stones from inside the cherries and put the outside part of them inside the pie, and throw the inside or stony part of the cherries away."

"Oh, good land!" cried the hedgehog, "no wonder I couldn't eat the pie. You see, I thought cherries were like peanuts. For you know you throw away the outside part of the peanut, and eat the inside."

"Yes, and cherries are just the opposite," said the rabbit, laughing again. "For you eat the outside of a cherry and throw away the pit or stone that is inside. Now, I'll make you a cherry pie."

"I wish you would," said the porcupine. "I'll go get the cherries."

So he went out in the orchard, and he shot his sharp stickery quills, like little arrows at the cherries on the tree, and they fell down, so he could pick them up in a basket. I mean the cherries fell down, though of course the quills did also though the hedgehog didn't pick them up.

And while he was doing that Uncle Wiggily was making the pie crust. He took flour and lard and water, and mixed them together, and then he put in other things — Oh, well, you just ask your mamma or the cook what they were, for I might get it wrong — and soon the pie crust was ready. Then Uncle Wiggily built a hot fire in the stove, and he waited for Mr. Hedgehog to come in with the cherries.

And pretty soon the porcupine came back with his basket full, and he and Uncle Wiggily shelled the peanuts — I mean the cherries — taking out the pits.

"Now I'll put them in the pie, and put sugar on them, bake it in the oven, and soon it will be done, and we can eat it," said the rabbit.

"Oh, joy!" cried the hedgehog. "That will be fine!"

So Uncle Wiggily put the cherries in the pie, and threw the pits away, and he put the pie in the oven, and then he and Mr. Hedgehog sat down to wait for it to bake. And oh, how delicious and scrumptious it did smell! if you will excuse me for saying so.

Well, in a little while, the pie was baked, and Uncle Wiggily took it from the oven.

"I can hardly wait to eat it!" cried the hedgehog, and just then there came a terribly loud knock on the door.

"Oh, maybe it's that bad fox come for some of my pie!" exclaimed the hedgehog. "If it is, I'll stick him full of stickery-stickers." But when he went to the door there stood old Percival, the circus dog, and he was crying as hard as he could cry.

"Come in," invited Uncle Wiggily. "Come in, and have some cherry pie, and you'll feel better." So Percival came in, and they all three sat down, and ate the cherry pie all up, and sure enough Percival did feel better, and stopped crying.

Then the circus dog and Uncle Wiggily stayed all night with Mr. Hedgehog, and they had more cherry pie next day, and it was very fine and sweet.

Now, if our cook makes some nice watermelon sandwiches, with maple syrup on them, for supper, I'll tell you in the next story about Uncle Wiggily and old dog Percival, and why Percival cried.

Story XVI

UNCLE WIGGILY AND PERCIVAL

Now I'm going to tell you, before I forget it, why old dog Percival was crying that time when he came to the little stone house where the hedgehog lived, and where Uncle Wiggily gave him some cherry pie. And the reason Percival was crying, was because he had stepped on a sharp stone, and hurt his foot.

"But I don't in the least mind now," said Percival, after he had eaten about sixty-'leven pieces of the pie. "My foot is all better."

"I should think that cherry pie would make almost anyone better," said the hedgehog, laughing with joy, for he felt better, too. "I know some bad boys to whom I'm going to give some cherry pie, and I hope it makes them better. And to think I threw away the good part of the cherries and cooked the stones in the pie. Oh, excuse me while I laugh again!"

And the hedgehog laughed so hard that he spilled some of the red cherry pie juice on his shirt front, but he didn't care, for he had another shirt.

Well, Uncle Wiggily and Percival, the old circus dog, stayed for some days at the home of the hedgehog, and they had cherry pie, or fritters with maple syrup, at almost every meal. Then, finally, Uncle Wiggily said:

"Well, I guess I must travel on. I can't find my fortune here. I must start off tomorrow."

"And I'll go with you," spoke Percival. "We'll go together, and see what we can find."

Well, he and Uncle Wiggily went on together for some time, and nothing happened, except that they met a poor pussy cat without any tail, and Uncle Wiggily gave her some of the pie. And the next day they met a cat and seven little kittens, and they all had tails, so they had to have some pie, too.

But one night, after Percival and Uncle Wiggily had been traveling all day, they came to a deep, dark, dismal woods.

"Oh, have we got to go through that forest?" asked the old gentleman rabbit, wrinkling up his ears — I mean his nose.

"I guess we have," replied the circus dog. "We may find our fortunes in there."

"It is a pretty dark spot to look for money, or fortunes," said the rabbit. "The best thing we can do is to look for a place to sleep, and in the morning we will hurry out of the woods."

Well, the two animal friends started into the grove of trees, and they hadn't gone very far before it got so dark that they couldn't see to go any farther. Oh, but it was black and lonesome and sort of scarylike! and Uncle Wiggily said:

"Let's stay here, Percival. We'll make a little bed under the trees to sleep in, and we'll build a fire to keep us warm, and cook a little supper."

So Percival thought that would be nice, and soon he and the rabbit had a cheerful little fire blazing, and then it wasn't quite so lonely. Only there was a big owl in a tree, and he kept hollering "Who? Who? Who?" and Percival thought it meant him, and Uncle Wiggily thought it meant him, and they were rather frightened, so they didn't either of them answer the owl, who kept on calling "Who? Who? Who?"

They were just cooking their supper, and cutting up the cherry pie, and putting it on some oak leaves for plates, and they had picked out a nice smooth stump for a table, when, all of a sudden, they heard a voice saying:

"Now you make a jump and grab the rabbit and I'll take the dog. Then we can carry them off to our dens, and that will be the last of them. Get ready now!"

"Did you hear that?" asked Uncle Wiggily of the circus dog.

"Indeed I did," replied Percival. "I wonder if it can be those owls?"

"It doesn't sound like them," said Uncle Wiggily. "I think it is a bad fox, or maybe two of them."

And just then they looked off through the woods, and by the light of the fire they saw two big, savage, ugly wolves. Oh, how their sharp teeth gleamed in the dancing flames, and how red their tongues were!

"Come on! Grab 'em both!" cried one savage wolf. "Grab the rabbit and the dog!"

"Sure! I'm with you!" growled the other savage wolf.

"Oh, what shall we do, Uncle Wiggily?" asked Percival. "They'll eat us up!

"Let me think a minute," said the rabbit. So he thought for maybe half a minute, and then exclaimed: "Oh! I know a good thing to do."

"What?" asked Percival. "Say it quickly, Uncle Wiggily, for those wolves are creeping up on us, and it's so dark we can't see to run away."

And surely enough, those wolves were sneaking up, with their red tongues hanging out longer than ever, for all the world just as if they had eaten cherry pie.

"We must do some funny tricks!" exclaimed Uncle Wiggily. "You know how, Percival, for you were once in a circus, and I learned some when I was with the monkey, and with Fido Flip-Flop. Do some tricks, and maybe these wolves will feel so good-natured that they won't bite us."

So brave Uncle Wiggily stood up on one ear and waved his feet in the air. Then he stood on his nose and turned a somersault. Next he went around and around as fast as a pinwheel, and he whistled a funny tune about a little rubber ball that flew into the air, and when it landed on the ground it would not stay down there.

But I wish you could have seen the tricks Percival did. He jumped through between Uncle Wiggily's long ears, and he walked on his hind legs, and on his front ones. Then he stood on his head, and he made believe he was begging for something to eat, and Uncle Wiggily fed him a carrot, and a piece of pie. Then he put a piece of bread on his nose, tossed it up into the air — tossed the bread, I mean, not his nose — and when it came down he caught it and ate it. Oh, it was great!

Well, those wolves were too surprised for anything. They had never seen tricks like those. First they smiled a bit. Then they smiled some more. Then one laughed, then the other laughed, and finally, when Uncle Wiggily and Percival took turns jumping over each other's backs, the wolves thought it so funny that they had to lie down on the leaves and roll over and over because they were laughing so hard.

And, of course, after that they didn't feel like hurting Uncle Wiggily or Percival. And just then the big alligator came along and chased the wolves away, so the rabbit and dog had no one to bother them except the alligator, and, as he had just had his supper, he wasn't hungry, so he didn't eat them.

So Uncle Wiggily and Percival went to sleep, and so must you, and if the vegetable man brings me a pumpkin Jack o' Lantern, with a pink ribbon on the end of the stem, I'll tell you in the next story about Uncle Wiggily in a well.

Story XVII

UNCLE WIGGILY IN A WELL

*W*ell, I didn't get the pumpkin Jack o' Lantern with the pink ribbon on, but someone mailed me an ice cream cone, so it's just as well. That is, I suppose it was an ice cream cone when it started on its journey, but when I got it there was only the cone part left. Maybe the postman took out the ice cream, with which to stick a stamp on the letter.

But there, I must tell you what happened to Uncle Wiggily after he and Percival did those tricks, and made the wolves laugh so hard. The rabbit and the circus dog stayed in the woods all that night, and nothing bothered them.

"Now, Percival, you make the coffee, and I'll spread the bread and butter for breakfast," said Uncle Wiggily the next morning.

"Where are you going to get the bread and butter?" asked the dog.

"Oh, I have it in my satchel," spoke the old rabbit, and, surely enough, he did have several large, fine slices. So he and Percival ate their breakfast, and then they started off again.

They hadn't gone very far before they met a grasshopper, who was limping along on top of a fence rail, and looking quite sad — I mean the grasshopper was looking sad, not the fence rail.

"What is the matter?" asked Uncle Wiggily, kindly. "Are you sad and lonesome because you can't have some cherry pie, or some bread and butter; or because you can't see any funny tricks? If you are, don't worry, Mr. Grasshopper, for Percival and I can give you something to eat, and also do some tricks to make you laugh."

"No, I am not sad about any of those things," replied the grasshopper, "but you see I gave a big jump over a large stone a little while ago, and I sprained my left hind leg. Now I can't jump anymore, and here it is Summer, and, of course, we grasshoppers have to hop, or we don't make any money."

"Oh, don't let a little thing like that worry you," spoke Uncle Wiggily. "I have some very nice salve, that a gentleman and his boy gave me when their automobile ran over me, and it cured my sore toe, so I think it will cure your left hind leg."

Then he put some salve on the grasshopper's leg, and in a little while it was much better.

"Now we must travel on again, to seek our fortune," said Uncle Wiggily. "Come, Percival."

"I will just do one little trick, to make the grasshopper feel better before we leave," said the circus dog, so he stood up on the end of his tail, and went around and around, and winked first one eye and then the other, it was too funny for anything, really it was.

Well, the alligator laughed at that — oh there I go again — I mean the grasshopper laughed, and then Uncle Wiggily and Percival went off together, very glad indeed that they had had a chance to do a kindness, even to a grasshopper.

Pretty soon they came to a place where there were two roads branching off, one to the right hand and the other to the left, like the letter "Y."

"I'll tell you what we'll do," said Percival, "you go to the right, Uncle Wiggily, and I'll go to the left, and, later on, we'll meet by the mill pond, and perhaps each of us may have found his fortune by that time."

"Good!" cried Uncle Wiggily. "We'll do it!"

So he went off one way, and the circus dog took the other path through the woods, and now I must tell you what happened to the old gentleman rabbit.

Uncle Wiggily went along for some time, and just as he got to a place where there was a large stone, all of a sudden out popped a big fat toad. And it wasn't a nice toad, either, but a bad toad.

"Hello, Uncle Wiggily," said the squatty-watty toad. "I haven't seen you in some time. I guess you must be getting pretty old. You can't jump as good as you once could, can you?"

"Of course, I can," exclaimed the rabbit, a bit pettishlike, for he didn't care to have even a toad think he couldn't jump as well as ever he could.

"I'd like to see you," went on the toad. "See if you jump from here over on that pile of leaves," and he pointed to them with his warty toes.

"I'll do it," exclaimed Uncle Wiggily. So he laid aside his crutch and his valise, gave a little run and a big jump, and then he came down kerthump on the pile of leaves.

But wait. Oh! I have something sad to tell you. That toad was only playing a trick on the rabbit, and those leaves were right over a big, deep, dark well. And as soon as Uncle Wiggily landed on the leaves he fell through, for there were no boards under them to cover up the well, and down, down, down he went, and if there had been water in the well he would have been drowned. But the well was dry, I'm glad to say. Still Uncle Wiggily had a great fall — almost like the tumble of Humpty-Dumpty.

"Ah, ha!" exclaimed the mean, squatty-squirmy toad. "Now you are in the well, and I'm going off, and tell the wolves, so they can come and get you out, and eat you. Ah, ha!" Oh! but wasn't that toad a most unpleasant one? You see, he used to work for the wolves, doing all sorts of mean things for them, and trapping all the animals he could for them.

So off the toad hopped, to call the wolves to come and get Uncle Wiggily, and the poor rabbit was left alone at the bottom of the well. He tried his best to get up, but he couldn't.

"I guess I'll have to stay here until the wolves come," he thought, sadly. "But I'll call for help, and see what happens." So he called: "Help! Help! Help!" as loudly as he could.

And all of a sudden a voice answered and asked:

"Where are you?"

"In the well," shouted Uncle Wiggily, and he was afraid it was the wolves coming to eat him. But it wasn't, it was the limpy grasshopper, and he tried to pull Uncle Wiggily out of the well, but, of course, he wasn't strong enough.

"But I'll get Percival, the circus dog, and he'll pull you out before the wolves come," said the grasshopper. "Now I have a chance to do you a kindness for the one you did me." So he hopped off, as his leg was nearly all better, and he found Percival on the left road and told him what had happened.

And, my! how that circus dog did rush back to help Uncle Wiggily. And he got him out of the well in no time, by lowering a long rope to him, and pulling the rabbit gentleman up, and then the rabbit and dog ran away, before the toad could come back with the savage wolves, who didn't get any supper out of the well, after all, and it served them right.

So that's all of this story, but I have some more, about the adventures of Uncle Wiggily, and next, in case the load of hay doesn't fall on my puppy-dog, and break off his curly tail, I'll tell you about Uncle Wiggily and Jennie Chipmunk.

Story XVIII

UNCLE WIGGILY AND JENNIE CHIPMUNK

*A*fter Uncle Wiggily had been pulled up out of the well by Percival, the old circus dog, and they had run far enough off so that the wolves couldn't get them, the rabbit and the grasshopper and Percival sat down on the ground to rest. For you see Uncle Wiggily was tired from having fallen down the well, and the grasshopper was tired from having run so fast to call back Percival, and of course Percival was tired from having pulled up the old gentleman rabbit. So they were all pretty well tired out.

"I'm sure I can't thank you enough for what you did for me," said Uncle Wiggily to Percival, and the grasshopper. "And as a little treat I'm going to give you some cherry pie that I made for the hedgehog."

So they ate some cherry pie, and then they felt better. And they were just going to travel on together again, when, all at once, there was a rustling in the bushes, and out flew Dickie Chip-Chip, the sparrow boy.

"Oh, my" cried Uncle Wiggily, wrinkling up his nose. "At first I thought you were a savage owl."

"Oh, no, I'm not an owl," said Dickie. "But I'm in a great hurry, and perhaps I made a noise like an owl. Percival, you must come back home to the Bow Wow house right away."

"Why?" asked Percival, sticking up his two ears so that he could hear better.

"Because Peetie Bow Wow is very ill with the German measles, and he wants to see you do some of your funny circus tricks," spoke Dickie. "He thinks that will make him better."

"Ha! I've no doubt that it will!" exclaimed Uncle Wiggily. "If I were not traveling about, seeking my fortune, I'd go back with you, Percival. I love Peetie Bow Wow, and Jackie, too."

"Oh, I'll go," said the grasshopper. "I will play Peetie a funny fiddle tune, on my left hind leg, and that may make him laugh."

"And Nellie and I will sail through the air, and go off to find some pretty flowers for him," said Dickie.

So the sparrow boy, the grasshopper and old Percival, the circus dog, started off together to see poor sick Peetie Bow Wow, leaving Uncle Wiggily there on the grass.

"Give my love to Peetie!" called the old gentleman rabbit after them, "and tell him that I'll come and see him as soon as I find my fortune."

Uncle Wiggily felt a little bit sad and lonely when his friends were gone, but he ate another piece of cherry pie, taking care to get none of the juice, on his blue necktie, and then he was a little happier.

"Now to start off once more," he said. "I wonder what will happen next? But I know one thing, I'm never going to do any jumping for any squatty old toads anymore."

So Uncle Wiggily traveled on and on, and when it came night he didn't have anyplace to sleep. But as it happened he met a kind old water snake, who had a nice house in an old pile of wood, and there the rabbit stayed until morning, when the water snake got him a nice breakfast of pond lilies, with crinkly eel-grass sauce on.

Pretty soon it was nearly noon that day, and Uncle Wiggily was about to sit down on a nice green mossy bank in the woods — not a toy bank with money in it, you understand, but a dirt-bank, with moss on it like a carpet. That's where he was going to sit.

"I think I'll eat my dinner," said the old gentleman rabbit as he opened his valise, and just then he heard a voice in the woods singing. And this was the song:

"Oh dear! I'm lost, I know I am,
I don't know what to do.
I had a big red ribbon, and
I had one colored blue.

But now I haven't got a one
Because a savage bear
Took both of them, and tied a string
Around my curly hair.

I wish I had a penny bright,
To buy a trolley car.
I'd ride home then, because, you see,
To walk it is too far."

"I guess that's someone in trouble, all right," said Uncle Wiggily, as he cautiously peeped through the bushes. "Though, perhaps, it is a little wolf boy, or a fox." But when he looked, whom should he see but little Jennie Chipmunk, and she was crying as hard as she could cry, so she couldn't sing anymore.

"Why, Jennie, what is the matter?" kindly asked Uncle Wiggily.

"Oh, I came out in the woods to gather acorns in a little basket for supper," she said, "and I guess I must have come too far. The first thing I knew a big bear jumped out of the bushes at me, and he took off both my nice, new hair ribbons and put on this old string."

And, sure enough, there was only just an old black shoestring on Jennie's nice hair.

"Where is that bear?" asked Uncle Wiggily, quite savage like. "Just tell me where he is, and I'll make him give you back those ribbons, and then I'll show you the way home."

"Oh, the bear ran off after he scared me," said the little chipmunk girl. "Please don't look for him, Uncle Wiggily, or he might eat you all up."

"Pooh!" exclaimed the old gentleman rabbit. "I'm not afraid of a bear. I have traveled around a great deal of late, and I have had many adventures. It takes more than a bear to scare me!"

"Oh, it does; does it?" suddenly cried a growly-scowly voice, and, would you believe me? right out from the bushes jumped that savage bear! And he had Jennie's blue ribbon tied on his left ear, and the red one tied on his right ear, and he looked too queer for anything. "I can't scare you; eh?" he cried to the rabbit. "Well, I'm just going to eat you, and that chipmunk girl all up, and maybe that will scare you!"

So he made a jump for Uncle Wiggily, but do you s'pose the rabbit gentleman was afraid? Not a bit of it. He knew what he was going to do.

"Quick, Jennie!" called Uncle Wiggily. "Get in front of me. I'll fix this bear all right." So Jennie got in front, and the rabbit turned his back on the bear, and, then Uncle Wiggily began scratching in the dirt with his sharp claws. My! how he did make the dirt fly. It was just like a regular rain-shower of sand and gravel.

And the dirt flew all over that bear; in his eyes and nose and mouth and ears, it went, and he sneezed, and he couldn't see out of his eyes, and he fairly howled. And by that time Uncle Wiggily had dug a big hole in the ground with his feet, and he and Jennie hid there until the bear ran off to get some water to wash the dirt off his face, and then the rabbit and the chipmunk girl came out safely.

Then Uncle Wiggily gave Jennie some pennies to buy two new hair ribbons, and he showed her the way home with her basket of acorns, and he himself went on with his travels. And he had another adventure the next day. Now in case a cowboy doesn't come along, and take my little pussy cat off to the wild west show I'll tell you next about Uncle Wiggily and the paper lantern.

Story XIX

UNCLE WIGGILY AND THE LANTERN

*A*fter Uncle Wiggily had taken Jennie Chipmunk home, so that the bear couldn't get her, as I told you about in the story before this one, the old gentleman rabbit walked on over the fields and through the woods, seeking his fortune. He looked everywhere for it; down in hollow stumps, behind big stones, and even in an old well, but you may be sure he didn't jump down anymore wells. No, I guess not!

"Ha! Here is a little brook!" exclaimed Uncle Wiggily, after a while, as he came to a small stream of water flowing over green, mossy stones, with a nice gurgling sound like an ice cream soda, "perhaps I may find my fortune here."

But he looked and he looked in the water without seeing anything but a goldfish.

"I might sell the goldfish for money," thought the fortune-hunting rabbit, "but it wouldn't be kind to take him out of the brook, so I won't. I'll look a little farther, on the other side."

Then, taking up his crutch and his valise, Uncle Wiggily gave a big jump, and leaped safely across the water. Then, once more, he traveled on. Pretty soon he came to a place where there was a tree, and on one branch of this tree there hung a funny round ball, that looked as if it was made of grey-colored paper. And there was a funny buzzing sound coming from it.

"Ha! Do you see that?" asked a big, fat hop-toad, as he suddenly bobbed up out of the grass. It was the same toad who had made the rabbit jump down in the leaf-covered well. "Do you see that?" asked the toad.

"Well, if you want to find your fortune, take a stick and hit that ball."

"Indeed I will not!" cried the old gentleman rabbit. "I know you and your tricks! That is a hornets' nest, and if I struck it they would fly out, and sting me. Oh, no! You can't catch me again. Now you go away, or I'll tell a policeman dog to arrest you."

So the toad knew it was of no use to try to fool Uncle Wiggily again, and he hopped away, scratching his warty back on a sharp stone.

Well, the old gentleman rabbit traveled on and on, and when it came night he wondered where he was going to stay, for he hadn't yet found his fortune and the weather looked as if it was going to rain. Then, all of a sudden, he heard voices calling like this:

"Come on, Nannie, you've got to blind your eyes now, and I'll go hide."

"All right, Billie," was the answer. "And after that we'll get Uncle Butter to tell us a story."

"I guess I know who those children are," thought Uncle Wiggily, though he had not yet seen them. "That's Billie and Nannie Goat talking," and surely enough it was, and, most unexpectedly the rabbit had come right up to the house where they lived, on the edge of the woods.

Well, you can just imagine how glad Billie and Nannie were to see Uncle Wiggily.

They danced all around him, and held him by the paws, and kissed him between his long ears, and Billie carried his satchel for him.

"Oh, we're so glad you are here!" they cried. "Mamma! Papa! Uncle Butter! Here is Uncle Wiggily!"

Well, the whole goat family was glad to see the rabbit-traveler, and after supper he told them of his adventures, and how he was out seeking his fortune.

And Billie and Nannie told what they had been doing, and Nannie showed how she could cut things out of paper, like the children do in the kindergarten class in school. She could make little houses, with smoke coming out of the chimney, and paper lanterns, and boxes, and, oh! ever so many things. The lanterns she made were especially fine, just like Chinese ones.

Then it came time to go to bed, and in the night a very strange thing happened, and I'm going to tell you all about it.

Along about 12 o'clock, when all was still and quiet, and when the little mice were beginning to think it was time for them to creep, creep out of their holes, and hunt for bread and cheese; about this time there sounded a queer noise down at the front door of the goat-house.

"Ha! What is that?" asked Mrs. Goat.

"I guess it was the cats," said Mr. Goat, getting ready to go to sleep again.

"No, I'm sure it was a burglar-fox!" said the lady goat. "Please get up and look."

Well, of course, Mr. Goat had to do so, after his wife asked him like that. So he poked his head out of the upstairs window, over the front door, and he called out:

"Who is down there?"

"I'm a burglar-fox!" was the answer. "I'm coming to rob you."

"Oh, my!" cried Mrs. Goat, when she heard that. "Get a gun, and shoot him, Mr. Goat."

And at that Billie and Nannie began to cry, for they were afraid of burglars, and Uncle Butter got up, and began looking for a whistle, with which to call a policeman dog, but he couldn't find it.

Then the burglar-fox started in breaking down the door, so that he could get in, and still Mr. Goat couldn't find his gun.

"Oh, we'll all be killed!" cried Mrs. Goat. "Oh, if someone would only help us!"

"Ha! I will help you!" cried Uncle Wiggily jumping out of bed. "I'll scare that fox so that he'll run away."

"But I can't find my gun," said Mr. Goat.

"No matter," answered the brave rabbit. "I can scare him with a paper lantern such as Nannie can make. Quick, Nannie, make me a big paper lantern."

Well, the little goat girl stopped crying then, and she got her paper, and her scissors, and the paste pot, and she began to make a paper lantern, as big as a water pail. Uncle Wiggily and Billie helped her. And all the while the burglar-fox was banging on the door, and crying out:

"Let me in! Let me in!"

"Quick! is the lantern ready?" Asked Uncle Wiggily, jumping around in a circle like "Ring Around the Rosie."

"Here it is," said Nannie. So the rabbit gentleman took it, all nicely made as it was, and inside of it he put a hot, blazing candle. And the lantern was so big that the candle didn't burn the sides of the paper.

Then Uncle Wiggily tied the lantern to a string, and he lowered it right down out of the window; down in front of the burglar-fox, and the hot candle in the lantern burned the fox's nose, and he thought it was a policeman climbing down out of a tree to catch him, and before you could count forty-'leven the bad burglar-fox ran away, and so he didn't rob the goats after all. And, oh! how thankful Nannie and Billie and their papa and mamma were to Uncle Wiggily.

Now, in case the little boy next door doesn't take our clothesline, to make a swing for his puppy dog, I'll tell you about Uncle Wiggily and the paper house in the following story.

Story XX

UNCLE WIGGILY AND THE PAPER HOUSE

*B*right and early next morning Uncle Wiggily got up, and he took a careful look around to see if there were any signs of the burglar-fox, about whom I told you in another story.

"I guess he's far enough off by this time," said Billie Goat, as he polished his horns with a green leaf.

"Yes, indeed," spoke Uncle Wiggily. "It is a good thing that Nannie knew how to make a paper lantern."

"Oh, I can make lots of things out of paper," said the little goat girl. "Our teacher in school shows us how. Why I can even make a paper house."

"Can you, indeed?" asked the old gentleman rabbit, as he washed his paws and face for breakfast. "Now I should dearly like to know how to make a paper house."

"Why?" asked Billie Goat, curious like.

"So that when I am traveling about, looking for my fortune, and night comes on, and I have no place to stay, then I could make me a paper house, and be all nice and dry in case it rained," replied the rabbit.

"Oh, but the water would soon soak through the paper," said Billie. "I know, for once I made a paper boat, and sailed it on the pond, and soon it was soaked through, and sank away down."

"Oh, but if I use that funny, greasy paper which comes inside cracker boxes — the kind with wax on it — that wouldn't wet through," spoke the rabbit as he went inside the goat-house with the children, for Mrs. Goat had called them in to breakfast.

"That would be just fine!" exclaimed Nannie, as she passed some apple sauce and oatmeal to Uncle Wiggily. "After breakfast I'll show you how to make a paper house."

Well, surely enough, as soon as breakfast was over, and before she and Billie had gone to school, Nannie showed the old gentleman rabbit how to make a paper house. You take some paper and some scissors, and you cut out the sides of the house and the roof, and you make windows and doors in these sides, and then you make a chimney, and you fasten them all together, with paste or glue, and, there you are. Isn't it easy?

And if you only make the paper house large enough, you can get inside of it and have a play party, and perhaps you can make paper dishes and knives and forks; but listen! If you make paper things to eat, like cake or cookies or anything like that, please only make-believe to eat them, for they are bad for the digestion if you *really* chew them.

"Well, I think I'll travel along now, and once more seek my fortune," said Uncle Wiggily, when Billie and Nannie were ready to go to school. So Mrs. Goat packed up for the rabbit a nice lunch in his valise, and Nannie gave him some waxed paper, that the rain wouldn't melt, and Billie gave his uncle a pair of scissors, and off Mr. Longears started.

Well, he traveled on and on, over the fields and through the woods, and across little brooks, and pretty soon it was coming on dark night, and the rabbit gentleman hadn't found his fortune.

"Now I wonder where I can stay tonight?" thought Uncle Wiggily, as he looked about him. He could see nothing but an old stump, which was not hollow, so he couldn't get inside of it, and the only other thing that happened to be there was a flat stone, and he couldn't get under that.

"I guess I must make me a paper house," said the old gentleman rabbit. "Then I can sleep in it in peace and quietness, and I'll travel on again in the morning."

So he got out the waxed paper, and he took the scissors, and, sitting down on the green grass, he cut out the sides and roof of the paper house. Then he made the chimney, and put it on the roof, and then he fastened the house together, and crawled inside, with his valise and his barber-pole crutch.

"I guess I won't make too many windows or doors," thought Uncle Wiggily, "for a savage bear or a burglar-fox might come along in the night, and try to get in."

So he only made one door, and one window in the house. But he made a little fireplace out of stones, and built a little fire in it, to cook his supper. But listen, you children must never, never make a fire, unless some big person is near to put it out in case it happens to run away, and chases after you, to catch you. Fires are dreadfully scary things for little folks, so please be careful.

Well, Uncle Wiggily cooked his supper, frying some carrots in a little tin frying pan he had with him, and then he said his prayers, and went to bed. Soon he was fast, fast asleep.

Well, in the middle of the night, Uncle Wiggily was awakened in his paper house by hearing a funny noise outside.

"Ha! I wonder what that can be?" he exclaimed, sitting up, and reaching out for his crutch. The noise kept on, "pitter-patter; pitter-patter-patter-pitter; pat-pit-pat-pit."

"Oh, that sounds like the toe nails of the burglar-fox, running around the house!" said the rabbit. Then he listened more carefully, and suddenly he laughed: "Ha! Ha!" Then he got up and looked out of the window. "Why, it's only the rain drops pit-pattering on the roof," he said. "Isn't it jolly to be in a house when it rains, and you can't get wet? After this every night I'm going to always build a waxed-paper house," said Uncle Wiggily.

So he listened to the rain drops, and he thought how nice it was not to be wet, and he went to sleep again. And pretty soon he woke up once more, for he heard another noise. This time it was a sniffing, snooping, woofing sort of a noise, and Uncle Wiggily knew that it wasn't the rain.

"I'm sure that's the burglar-fox," he said. "What shall I do? He can smash my paper house with his teeth and claws, and then eat me. I should have built a wooden house. But it's too late now. I know what I'll do. I'll dig a cellar underneath my paper house, and I'll hide there, in case that fox smashes the roof."

So Uncle Wiggily got up very softly, and right in the middle of the dirt floor of his paper house he began to burrow down to dig a cellar. My, how his paws made the sand and gravel fly, and soon he had dug quite a large cellar, in which to hide.

And all this time the sniffing, snooping sound kept on, until, all of a sudden a voice cried:

"Let me in!"

"Who are you?" asked Uncle Wiggily.

"I'm the bad alligator," was the answer, "and if you don't let me in, I'll smash down your paper house with one swoop of my scalery-ailery tail."

"You can't come in!" cried the rabbit, and then that bad alligator gave one swoop of his tail, and smashed Uncle Wiggily's nice paper house all to pieces!

But do you s'pose the rabbit was there? No, indeed. He just grabbed up his crutch and valise, and ran down into his cellar as far and as fast as he could run, just as the roof fell in. And the cellar wasn't big enough for the alligator to get in, and so he had to stay outside, and he couldn't get Uncle Wiggily.

And then it rained, and thundered and lightninged, and the alligator got scared, and ran off, but the rabbit gentleman was safe down in his cellar, and he didn't get a bit wet, and went to sleep there for the rest of the night. Now, please go to bed, and in case my toothbrush, doesn't go out roller skating, and fall down and get bald-headed, I'll tell you next about Uncle Wiggily and the paper boat.

Story XXI

UNCLE WIGGILY IN A PAPER BOAT

*W*hen the morning dawned, after he had slept all night in the cellar under his paper house, that the alligator, with his swooping scalery-ailery tail, had knocked down, Uncle Wiggily awakened, brushed the dirt from his ears, and crawled out.

"My!" he exclaimed as he saw the paper house all flat on the ground, like a pancake, "Nannie Goat would certainly be sorry to see this. But I suppose it can't be helped. Anyhow, it's a good thing that I am not squashed as flat as that house is. Now I'll see about my breakfast, and then I'll travel on again."

So the old gentleman rabbit got his breakfast, eating almost the last piece of the cherry pie, which he had left from the time when he made some for the hedgehog, and then, taking his crutch, striped red, white and blue, like a barber pole, off he started.

Well, pretty soon, in a little while, not so very long, Uncle Wiggily came to a pond of water, and, looking down into it, he saw the most beautiful goldfish that you can imagine. It was a big fish, too, and the scales on it were as round as gold dollars.

"My!" exclaimed the rabbit. "If I had that fish, and I could take him to a jewelry shop, and sell him, I would get so much money that my fortune would be made, and I wouldn't have to travel any farther. But I guess the fish would rather stay in the pond than in a jewelry shop."

"Indeed, I would," answered the fish, looking up. "And I am glad you are so kind as to be thoughtful of my feelings. Perhaps I may be able to help you, some day."

And with that the fish dived away down under the water, after calling good-bye to the rabbit, and then Uncle Wiggily hopped on, and he didn't think anymore about the goldfish, until some time after that.

Well, as soon as the elephant had his trunk packed — Oh, hold on, if you please. I wonder what's the matter with me? There's no elephant in this story. He comes in it about five pages farther on.

Well, after traveling for several hours, Uncle Wiggily ate his dinner, then he hopped on some more, and he looked all around for his fortune, but he couldn't find it. Then it began to get dark, and he wondered where he could stay that night.

"I might build a paper house," he said, "but if I do the alligator might come along and smash it, and this time he would probably catch me. I wonder what I'd better do?"

So he looked ahead, and there he saw a stream of water. It was quite a wide brook, but on the other side of it he saw a nice little wooden house, that no one lived in.

"Now, if I could only get over there I'd be safe," said the old gentleman rabbit. "I guess I'll wade across."

Well, he started to do so, but he soon found that the water was too deep for him to wade. It was over his head.

"I'll have to swim across," said Uncle Wiggily.

But, as soon as he got ready to do that, he found himself in more trouble. For he couldn't carry his crutch and valise across with him if he swam, and he didn't like to leave them on the shore, for fear the alligator would get them.

"Oh, I certainly am in great trouble," said the rabbit. "It's getting darker and darker, and I have no place to stay. I haven't even any paper with which to make me a paper house, but if I could only get across to the wooden house, I'd be safe."

And, just as he spoke, there came a little puff of wind, and lo and behold! a nice piece of paper was blown right down out of a tree, where it had been caught on a branch. Right at Uncle Wiggily's side it fell; that paper did.

"Oh, joy!" the rabbit gentleman cried. "Here is paper to make me a house with." But when he looked more closely at it, he saw that it wasn't big enough for a house, and it wasn't the kind of paper that would keep out the rain, either.

"That will never do," said Uncle Wiggily, sadly. "Ah! But I have an idea. I will make me a paper boat, as Billie Goat once did, and in the boat I'll sail across the stream, and sleep in the little wooden house."

So he folded up the paper, first like a soldier's hat, and then like a fireman's hat, and then he pulled on the two ends, and, presto change! he had a paper boat. Then he took his crutch, and stuck it up in the middle of the boat, and put a piece of paper on the crutch, and he had a sail. Then he put the boat in the water, and got in it himself. I mean he got in the boat, not the water — with his valise.

"Here we go!" cried the old gentleman rabbit, and he shoved the boat out from the shore. The wind caught in the little paper sail, and away Uncle Wiggily went, as fine as fine could be.

"I'll soon be on the other shore," he said, and just then he looked down, and he saw some water coming inside the boat. "Hum! That's bad," he cried. "I'm afraid my boat is leaking."

The wind blew harder, and the boat went faster, but more water came in, for you see the paper was sort of melting, and falling apart, like an ice cream cone, for it wasn't the waxed kind of paper from the inside of cracker boxes — the kind that water won't hurt.

Well, the boat began to sink, and the water came up to Uncle Wiggily's knees, and then, all of a sudden there was a funny sound on shore, a snipping snooping woofing-woofing sound, and into the water jumped the alligator with the skiller-scalery, swooping tail.

"Now I've got you!" he cried, snapping his jaws at the poor old gentleman rabbit. And really it did seem as if Uncle Wiggily would be eaten up. But you never can tell what is going to happen in this world; never indeed.

All of a sudden, just as the paper boat was melting all to pieces, and Uncle Wiggily was trying, as best he could, to swim to shore with his crutch and valise, and just as the alligator was going to grab him, along came the big, kind goldfish.

"Jump on my back, Uncle Wiggily!" cried the fish, and the rabbit did so, in the twinkling of an eye. And before the alligator could grab Uncle Wiggily, the goldfish swam to shore with him, and he was safe. And the alligator got some soap in his eye, from washing his face too hard, and went sloshing away as mad as could be, but it served him right. And Uncle Wiggily slept safely in the wooden house all night, and dreamed about finding a gold dollar.

Now in case the banana man brings me some pink oranges for the elephant's little boy, I'll tell you in another story about Uncle Wiggily and the mud pie.

Story XXII

UNCLE WIGGILY AND THE MUD PIE

*U*ncle Wiggily slept very soundly that night in the little wooden house, across on the other side of the brook, where the alligator tried to catch him, but didn't. And when he awakened in the morning the rabbit traveler wondered what he was going to have for breakfast. But he didn't wonder very long.

For, as soon as he had gotten up, and had washed his paws and face, and combed out his ears — oh, dear me — I mean his whiskers — as soon as he had done that, he heard a knock on the door.

"Oh, my, suz dud and a bottle of milk!" exclaimed the old gentleman rabbit. "I hope that isn't the scary-flary alligator again."

So he peeped out of the window, but to his surprise, he didn't see anyone.

"I'm sure I heard a knock," he said, "but I guess I was mistaken."

Well, he was going over to his valise to see if it had in it anything to eat, when the knock again sounded on the door.

"No, I wasn't mistaken," said Uncle Wiggily. "I wonder who that can be? I'll peep, and find out."

So he hid behind the window curtain, and kept a close watch, and the first things he saw were some little stones flying through the air. And they hit against the front door with a rattlety-bang, and it was these stones that had made the sound that was like a knock.

"Oh! it must be some bad boys after me," thought the poor old gentleman rabbit. "My! I do seem to be having a dreadful time seeking my fortune. There is always some kind of trouble."

And then more stones came through the air, and banged on the door and this time Uncle Wiggily saw that they came from the stream, and, what is more, he saw the goldfish throwing the stones and pebbles out of the brook with his tail. Then the rabbit knew it was all right, for the goldfish was a friend of his, so he ran out.

"Were you throwing stones at the house?" asked Uncle Wiggily.

"Yes," replied the fish, "it was the only way in which I could knock on your door. You see I dare not leave the water, and I wanted you to know that I had some breakfast for you."

And with that the kind goldfish took a little basket, made of water-cress, from off his left front fin, and handed Uncle Wiggily the basket, not his fin, for he needed that to swim with.

"You'll find some cabbage-salad with snorkery-snickery ell-grass dressing on it, some water-lily cake, and some moss covered eggs for your breakfast," said the fish. "And I wish you good luck on your travels today."

"Thank you very much," said Uncle Wiggily, "and I am very much obliged to you for saving me from the alligator last night."

"Pray do not mention it," spoke the fish most condescendingly. "I always like to help my friends." And with that he swam away, and Uncle Wiggily ate his breakfast, and then, taking his crutch and valise, he set off on his travels again.

He hopped on for some time, and finally he came to a place where there were some high, prickly bramble-briar bushes.

"I will rest here in their shade a bit," thought the old gentleman rabbit, "and then I will go on."

So he sat down, and, as the sun was quite warm, he fell asleep before he knew it. But he was suddenly awakened by a hissing sound, just like when steam comes out of the parlor radiator on a frosty night. Then a voice cried:

"Now I've got you!"

Uncle Wiggily looked up, and there was a big snake, just going to grab him. But do you s'pose the rabbit waited for that snake? Not a bit of it. Catching up his crutch and valise, he gave one tremendous and extraordinary springery-spring, and over the prickery stickery briar and bramble bushes he went, flying through the air, and the snake couldn't get him.

But when Uncle Wiggily came down on the other side of the bushes! Oh, my! that was a different story. For where do you imagine he landed? Where, indeed, but right in the middle of a big mud pie that two little hedgehog boys were making there. Yes, sir, right into the middle of that squasher-squawshery mud pie fell Uncle Wiggily.

Oh! How the mud splashed up! It went all over the rabbit, and some got on the two little hedgehog boys.

Well, they were as surprised as anything when they saw a nice old gentleman rabbit come down in the middle of their pie, and at first they thought he had done it on purpose.

"Let's stick him full of our stickery-stockery quills," said one hedgehog boy.

"Yes, and then let's pull his ears," said the other hedgehog boy. But, mind you, they didn't really mean anything bad, only, perhaps, they thought Uncle Wiggily was a savage fox, or a little white bear.

"Oh, boys, I'm sorry!" said the old gentleman rabbit as soon as he could dig the mud out of his mouth.

"What made you do it?" asked the biggest hedgehog boy, wiping some mud out of his eye.

"Yes, our pie is all spoiled," said his brother, "and we were just going to bake it."

"Oh, it is too bad!" said Uncle Wiggily, sorrowfully, "but you see I had to get away from that snake, and I didn't have time to look where I was jumping. I'm glad, though, that I left the snake on the other side of the bushes."

"So are we," said the two hedgehog boys.

"But you didn't leave me there. I'm here!" suddenly cried a voice, and out wiggled the snake again. He started to catch the rabbit, but those two brave hedgehog boys grabbed up a lot of mud, and plastered it in that snake's eyes so that he couldn't see, and he had to wiggle down to the pond to wash it out.

Then Uncle Wiggily and the boys were safe, and he helped them to make another mud pie, with stones in for raisins, and he gave them some of his real cherry pie, and oh! how they liked it! Then they were all happy, and Uncle Wiggily stayed at the hedgehog's house until the next morning.

Now, in case the little girl in the next house brings me a watermelon ice cream cone with a rose on top, I'll tell you on the next page about Uncle Wiggily and the elephant.

Story XXIII

UNCLE WIGGILY AND THE ELEPHANT

*U*ncle Wiggily didn't sleep very well at the hedgehog's house that night, and the reason for it was this: You see they didn't have many beds there, and first the rabbit gentleman lay down with the smallest little porcupine boy, in his bed.

But pretty soon, along about in the middle of the night, this little boy got to dreaming that he was a rubber ball. And he rolled over in the bed, and he rolled up against Uncle Wiggily, and the stickery-stickers from the little hedgehog chap stuck in the old gentleman rabbit.

"Oh, dear!" cried Uncle Wiggily, "I think I'll have to go and sleep with your brother Jimmie."

So he went over to the other hedgehog boy's bed, but land sakes flopsy-dub and a basket of soap bubbles!

As soon as the rabbit got in there that other hedgehog chap began to dream that he was a jumping jack, and so he jumped up and down, and he jumped on top of Uncle Wiggily, and stuck more stickery-stickers in him, until at last the rabbit got up and said:

"Oh, dear, I guess I'll have to go to sleep on the floor."

So he did that, putting his head on his satchel for a pillow and pulling his red-white-and-blue-striped-barber-pole crutch over him for a cover. And, in the morning, he felt a little better.

"Well, I think I will travel on once more," said Uncle Wiggily after a breakfast of strawberries, and mush and milk. "I may find my fortune today."

The hedgehog boys wanted him to stay with them, and make more mud pies, or even a cherry one, but the rabbit gentleman said he had no time. So off he went over hills and down dales, and along through the woods.

Pretty soon, not so very long, just as Uncle Wiggily was walking behind a big rock, as large as a house, he heard someone crying. Oh, such a loud crying voice as it was, and the old rabbit gentleman was a bit frightened.

"For it sounds like a giant crying," he said to himself. "And if it's a giant he may be a bad one, who would hurt me. I guess I'll run back the other way."

Well, he started to run, but, just as he did so, he heard the voice crying again, and this time it said:

"Oh, dear me! Oh, if someone would only help me! Oh, I am in such trouble!"

"Come, I don't believe that is a giant after all," thought the rabbit. "It may be Sammie Littletail, who has grown to be such a big boy that I won't know him anymore." So he took a careful look, but instead of seeing his little rabbit nephew, he saw a big elephant, sitting on the ground, crying as hard as he could cry.

Now, you know, when an elephant cries it isn't like when you cry once in a great while, or when baby cries every day. No, indeed! An elephant cries so very many tears that if you don't have a water pail near you, to catch them, you may get your feet wet; that is, if you don't have on rubbers.

Well, that's the way it was this time. The elephant was crying big, salty tears, about the size of rubber balls, and they were rolling down from his eyes and along his trunk, which was like a fire engine hose, until there was quite a little stream of water flowing down the hill toward the rabbit.

"Oh, please don't cry anymore!" called Uncle Wiggily.

"Why not?" asked the elephant, sadlylike, and he cried harder than before.

"Because if you do," replied the rabbit, "I will have to get a pair of rubber boots, in which to wade out to see you."

"I'll try to stop," said the big animal, but, instead, he cried harder than before, boo-hooing and hoo-booing, until you would have thought it was raining, and Uncle Wiggily wished he had an umbrella.

"Why, whatever is the matter?" asked the rabbit.

"Oh, I stepped on a tack," answered the elephant, "and it is sticking in my foot. I can't walk, and I can't dance and I can't get back to the circus. Oh, dear! Oh, dear me, suz-dud and a red balloon! Oh, how miserable I am!"

"Too bad," said Uncle Wiggily. "Was it a large tack that you stepped on?"

"Was it?" asked the elephant, sort of painfullike. "Why, it feels as big as a dishpan in my foot. Here, you look, and perhaps you can pull it out."

He raised up one of his big feet, which were about as large as a washtub full of clothes, on Monday morning, and he held it out to Uncle Wiggily.

"Why, I can't see anything here," said the rabbit, looking at the big foot through his spectacles.

"Oh, dear! It's there all right!" cried the elephant. "It feels like two wash tubs now," and he began to cry some more.

"Here! Hold on, if you please!" shouted Uncle Wiggily. "I'll have to make a boat, if you keep on shedding so many tears, for there will be a lake here. Wait, I'll look once more."

So he looked again, and this time he saw just the little, tiniest, baby-tack you can imagine — about the size of a pinhead — sticking in the elephant's foot.

"Wait! I have it! Was this it?" suddenly asked the rabbit, as he took hold of the tack in his paw and pulled it out.

"That's it!" exclaimed the elephant, waving his trunk. "It's out! Oh, how much better I feel. Whoop-de-doodle-do!" and then he felt so fine that he began to dance. Then, all of a sudden, he began to cry once more.

"Why, what in the world is the matter now?" asked Uncle Wiggily, wishing he had a pail, so that he might catch the elephant's salty tears.

"Oh, I feel so happy that I can't help crying, because my pain is gone!" exclaimed the big creature. Then he cried about forty-'leven bushels of tears, and a milk bottle full besides, and there was a little pond around him, and Uncle Wiggily was in it up to his neck.

Then, all of a sudden, in came swimming the alligator, right toward the rabbit.

"Ah, now I'll get you!" cried the skillery-scalery beast.

"No you won't!" shouted the elephant, "Uncle Wiggily is my friend!" So he put his trunk down in the water, and sucked it all up, and then he squirted it over the trees. That left the alligator on dry land, and then the elephant grabbed the alligator up in his strong trunk, and tossed him into the briar bushes, scalery-ailery tail and all, and the alligator crawled away after a while.

So that's how Uncle Wiggily was saved from the alligator by the crying elephant, and the rabbit and elephant traveled on together for some days. Now, as I see the sand man coming, I must stop.

But, in case I don't fall into the washtub with my new suit on, and get it all colored sky-blue-pink, so I can't go to the picnic, I'll tell you next about Uncle Wiggily and the cherry tree.

Story XXIV

UNCLE WIGGILY AND THE CHERRY TREE

*U*ncle Wiggily Longears and the crying elephant were walking along together one day, talking about the weather, and wondering if it would rain, and all things like that. Only the elephant wasn't crying anymore, for the rabbit had pulled the tack that was hurting him, out of the big beast's foot, you remember.

"We'll travel on together to find our fortune, and look for adventures," said the elephant, as he capered about, and stood on his hind legs, because he felt so jolly. "Won't we have fun, Uncle Wiggily?"

"Well, we may," spoke the old gentleman rabbit, "but I don't see how we are going to carry along on our travels enough for us to eat. Of course, *I* don't need much, but *you* are such a big chap that you will have to have quite a lot, and my valise is small."

"Don't worry about that," replied the elephant. "Of course you might think I could carry a lot of pie and cake and bread and butter in my trunk, but really I can't you know, for about all that my trunk will hold is water. However, I think I can pick what hay and grass I want from along the road."

"Yes, and perhaps we may meet a man with a hot peanut wagon, once in a while," suggested Uncle Wiggily, "and he may give you some peanuts."

"Oh, joy! I hope he does!" cried the big fellow. "I just love hot peanuts!" Well, they went on together for some time, when, all of a sudden a man jumped out from behind the bushes, and exclaimed:

"Ha, Mr. Elephant! I've been looking for you. Now you come right back with me to the circus where you belong." And he went up to the elephant and took hold of his trunk.

"Oh, I don't want to go," whined the tremendous creature. "I want to stay with Uncle Wiggily, and have some fun."

"But you can't," said the man. "You are needed in the circus. A lot of boys and girls are waiting in the tent, to give you peanuts and popcorn."

"Well, then, I s'pose I'd better go back," sighed the wobbly animal with the long tusks. "I'll see you again, Uncle Wiggily." So the elephant said good-bye to the rabbit, and went back to the circus with the man, while the rabbit gentleman hopped on by himself.

He hadn't gone very far before he heard a loud "Honk-honk!" in the bushes.

"Oh, there is another one of those terrible automobiles!" thought the rabbit. But it wasn't at all. No, it was Grandfather Goosey Gander, and there he sat on a flat stone, "honk-honking" through his yellow bill as hard as he could, and, at the same time crying salty tears that ran down his nose, making it all wet.

"Why, whatever is the matter?" asked Uncle Wiggily, as he went up to his friend, the duck-drake gentleman. "Have you stepped on a tack, too?"

"No, it isn't that," was the answer. "But I am so sick that I don't know what to do, and I'm far from my home, and from my friends, the Wibblewobble family, and, oh, dear! it's just awful."

"Let me look at your tongue," said the rabbit, and when Grandfather Goosey Gander stuck it out, Uncle Wiggily said:

"Why, you have the epizootic very bad. Very bad, indeed! But perhaps I can cure you. Let me see, I think you need some bread and butter, and a cup of catnip tea. I'll make you some."

So Uncle Wiggily made a little fire of sticks, and then he found an empty tin tomato can, and he boiled some water in it over the fire, and made the catnip tea. Then he gave some to Grandfather Goosey Gander, together with some bread and butter.

"Well, I feel a little better," said the old gentleman duck-drake, when he had eaten, "but I am not well yet. It seems to me that if I could have some cherry pie I would feel better."

"Perhaps you would," agreed Uncle Wiggily, "but, though I know how to make nice cherry pie, and though I made some for the hedgehog, I don't see any cherry trees around here, so I can't make you one. There are no cherry trees."

"Yes, there is one over there," said the duck-drake, and he waved one foot toward it, while he quacked real faint and sorrowfullike.

"Sure enough, that *is* a cherry tree," said Uncle Wiggily, as he hopped over and looked at it. "And the cherries are ripe, too. Now, if I could only get some of them down I could make a cherry pie, and cure Grandfather Goosey Gander."

But it wasn't easy to get the cherries off the tree, and Uncle Wiggily couldn't climb up after them. So he sat down and looked up at them, hoping some would fall off the stems. But none did.

"Oh, dear, I wonder how I'm going to get them?" sighed the rabbit. "Perhaps I can knock off some with a stone."

So he threw a stone, but no cherries came down. The stone did, though, and hit Uncle Wiggily on the nose, making him sneeze.

"Stones are no good!" exclaimed the rabbit. "I'll throw up my crutch." So he threw that into the tree, but it brought no cherries down, and the crutch, in falling, nearly hit Grandfather Goosey Gander, and almost gave him the measles and mumps.

"Well, I'll try and see what throwing up my valise will do," said the rabbit, and he tossed up the satchel, but bless you, that stayed up in the tree, and didn't come down at all, neither did any cherries.

"Oh, I'll have to give up," said Uncle Wiggily. "I'm afraid you can't have any cherry pie, Grandfather Goosey."

"Oh, then I'll never get well," said the old duck-drake gentleman sorrowfully.

"Yes, you will, too!" suddenly cried out a voice, and out from the bushes ran the elephant. "I'll pick the cherries off the tree with my long, nosey trunk," he said, "and you can make all the pie you want to, Uncle Wiggily."

"Why, I thought you went back to the circus," said the rabbit.

"No, I ran away from the man," spoke the elephant. Then he reached up with his long nose, and he picked a bushel of red, ripe, sweet delicious cherries in less than a minute. Then he pulled down Uncle Wiggily's valise out of the tree and then the old gentleman rabbit made three cherry pies. One for Grandfather Goosey Gander, and another, a tremendous big one, as large as a washtub, for the elephant, and a little one for himself. Then they ate their pies, and the old gentleman duck-drake got well almost at once. So all three of them traveled on together, to help the rabbit seek his fortune.

Now in case the ice cream man brings some nice, hot roast chestnuts for our canary bird, I'll tell you in another story about Uncle Wiggily, and Grandfather Goosey Gander.

Story XXV

UNCLE WIGGILY AND GRANDPA GOOSEY

One day, not very long after the elephant had picked the cherries off the tree, so that Uncle Wiggily could make the cherry pies for Grandpa Goosey, the three friends were traveling along together through a deep, dark, dismal woods.

"Where are we going?" asked the elephant, who had run away from the circus man to travel by himself.

"Oh, to some place where we may find our fortune," said the old gentleman rabbit.

"I would much rather find some snails to eat," said Grandfather Goosey Gander, the old gentleman duck, as I shall call him for short. "For I am very hungry."

"What's that?" cried the rabbit. "Hungry after the nice pie I made for you?"

"Oh, that was some time ago. I could eat another pie right now," spoke the old duck. But there wasn't any pie for him, so he had to eat a cornmeal sandwich with watercress salad on, and Uncle Wiggily ate some carrots and cabbage, and the elephant ate a lot of grass from a field — oh! a terrible lot — about ten bushels, I guess.

Then, all at once, as they were walking along over a bridge, a man suddenly jumped out from behind a tree, and cried:

"Ah, ha! Now you won't get away from me, Mr. Elephant. This time I am surely going to take you back to the circus." And with that he threw a rope around the elephant's trunk, and led him away. The elephant cried so many tears that there was a muddy puddle right near the bridge, and the big animal begged to be allowed to stay with Uncle Wiggily and Grandpa Goosey Gander, but the man said it could not be done.

"Well, then, you and I will have to go on together," said the old gentleman rabbit to the duck, after a bit. "Perhaps we may find our fortune."

"I think I could make money calling out 'honk-honk!' on an automobile," said the grandfather. "Jimmie Wibblewobble once did that for a man. I think I'll look for a nice automobile gentleman to work for, and if I get money enough we'll be rich."

Well, he looked and looked, but no one seemed to want an old duck for an auto horn, and the rabbit and Grandfather Goosey Gander kept on traveling together, over the fields and through the woods.

Pretty soon they came to a place where a June bug was sitting on the edge of a stone wall, buzzing his wings.

"Let's ask him where we can find our fortunes," said Uncle Wiggily. So they asked the June bug.

"Well," replied the buzzing creature, "I am not sure, but a little way from here are two roads. One or the other might bring you to your fortune. One goes to the right, the other to the left hand."

"We will take the left hand road," said Uncle Wiggily. "We will go down that for some distance, and if we do not find a pot of gold, or some ice cream cones at the end of it, we will come back, and try the other road."

So Uncle Wiggily and Grandfather Goosey Gander went down the left road. On and on they went, walking in the dust when there was any dust, and in the mud when there was any mud. But they didn't find any gold.

"Oh, let's go back and try the other road," said the rabbit gentleman after a bit. "Perhaps that will be better."

So back they went, stopping on the way to look at a big apple tree, to see if there were any ripe apples on it. But there was none, so they didn't eat any. And I hope you children do the same this summer. Never eat green apples, never, never, never! Wait until they are ripe.

Well, by and by, after a while, not so very long, Uncle Wiggily, who was hopping along on his crutch, suddenly exclaimed:

"Oh, I've lost my valise! What shall I do? I can't go on without it, for it has our lunch in it."

"I think you left it under the green-apple tree," said the duck. "You had better go back for it, and I will wait here in the shade," for Grandpa Goosey knew the rabbit could hop faster than he could waddle.

Back Uncle Wiggily started, and, surely enough, he found his valise under the apple tree, where he had forgotten it. He picked it up, and was walking along with it back to where Grandfather Goosey Gander was waiting for him when, all of a sudden, out from behind a stump came Jennie Chipmunk, with a basket of popcorn balls.

"Oh, Uncle Wiggily!" she exclaimed. "Don't you want to buy some popcorn balls? Our church is having a little fair, and we are all trying to earn some money. I am selling popcorn, to help the little heathen children buy red-colored handkerchiefs."

"Of course, I'll take some," said the old gentleman rabbit, "popcorn balls, I mean — not children, or hankerchiefs," he said quickly. So he bought a pink one, and a white one, and a chocolate colored one, popcorn balls you know — not children — and put them in his valise.

Then Uncle Wiggily sent his love to Sammie and Susie Littletail, by Jennie Chipmunk, and off he started to go back to where Grandfather Goosey Gander was waiting for him.

Well, something terrible was happening to the poor old gentleman duck, and I'll tell you all about it. No sooner had the rabbit gotten near the shady tree under which the grandfather gentleman was resting, than he heard a cry:

"Help! Help! Help!" called the duck. "Oh, help me quickly, somebody!"

"What is the matter?" asked Uncle Wiggily, limping along as fast as he could.

"Oh, a bad snake has caught me!" cried the duck. "He has wound himself around my legs, and I can't walk, and he is going to eat me up! He jumped on me out of the bushes. He will eat me!"

"He shall never do that!" cried the rabbit, bravely. "I will save you." So he ran up to that snake, but the snake stuck out his tongue, like a fork, at the rabbit, and Uncle Wiggily was frightened. Then he tried to hit the snake with a stick, but the crawly creature hid down behind Grandfather Goosey, and so got out of the way.

"I have it!" suddenly cried Uncle Wiggily. "The popcorn balls. Snakes love them! I'll make him eat them, and then he'll let Grandpa Goosey go." So from his valise the brave rabbit took the red and the white and the chocolate colored popcorn balls, and he rolled them along the ground, close to the snake's nose. And the snake smelled them, and he was so hungry for them that he uncoiled himself from Grandfather Goosey's legs, and let the old gentleman duck go. And the snake chased after the corn balls and ate them all up, and then he didn't want anything more for a long while, and he went to sleep for six months and dreamed about turning into a hoop, and so he didn't bother anybody.

So that's how Uncle Wiggily saved the duck, and next, in case the pretty baby across the street doesn't fall down and bump its nose, I'll tell you about Uncle Wiggily and the ice cream cones.

Story XXVI

UNCLE WIGGILY'S ICE CREAM CONES

*I*t didn't take Uncle Wiggily and Grandfather Goosey Gander long to get away from the place where the bad snake was, let me tell you, even if the crawly creature had eaten three popcorn balls, and would sleep for six months.

"This is no place for us," said the rabbit. "We must see if we can't find our fortune somewhere else."

"I believe you," spoke Grandfather Goosey, rubbing his yellow legs, where the snake had wound tight around him like a clothesline. "We'll look for a place in which to stay tonight, and we'll see what we can find tomorrow."

Well, they hurried on for some time, and pretty soon it began to get dark, and they couldn't find anyplace to stay.

"I guess I'll have to dig a hole in the ground, and make a burrow," said the rabbit.

"Oh, but I couldn't stay underground," said the duck. "I'm used to sleeping in a wooden house."

"That's so," said Uncle Wiggily. "Well, if I had some paper I could make you a paper house, but I haven't any, so I don't know what to do."

And just then, away in the air, there sounded a voice saying:

"Caw! Caw! Caw!"

"Ha! That's a crow," exclaimed Uncle Wiggily. "There must be green corn that is ready to pull up somewhere around here."

"There is," said the black crow, flying down. "I know a nice field of corn that a farmer has planted, and tomorrow I am going to pick some."

"But aren't you afraid of the scarecrow?" asked the duck.

"No; I'm not," said the crow. "The scarecrow is only some old clothes stuffed with straw, and it is set out in the field to drive us crows away. We're not a bit afraid of it. Would you be?"

"No, of course not," answered Grandfather Goosey Gander. "But then, you see, I'm not a crow — the scary figure wasn't meant for me."

"Then you can stay in one of the pockets of the scarecrow's coat all night," said the crow. "It will be a good place for you to sleep."

"The very thing!" cried Uncle Wiggily. So that night he dug himself a little house under the ground, and the duck gentleman flew up, and got inside the pocket of the old coat which the scarecrow figure wore, and there the duck stayed all night, sleeping very soundly.

"Well, now we'll travel on again," said Uncle Wiggily, the next morning after breakfast. So he and Grandfather Goosey started off. Well, pretty soon it became hotter and hotter, for the sun was just beaming down as hard as it could, and Uncle Wiggily exclaimed:

"I know what would taste good! An ice cream cone for each of us. Wait here, grandfather, and I'll get two of them."

"Fine!" cried the grandfather duck. "But you seem to do all the hopping around, Uncle Wiggily. Why can't I go, while you rest?"

"Oh, I don't in the least mind going," replied the kind rabbit. "Besides, while I do not say it to be proud, and far be it from me to boast, I can go a little faster than you can in one hop. So I'll go."

And go he did, leaving his valise in charge of Grandfather Goosey, who sat down with it, under a shady tree. Pretty soon the old gentleman rabbit came to a little ice cream store, that stood beside the road, right near a little pond of water, where the ice-cream-man could wash his dishes when he had to make them clean.

"I'll have two, nice, big, cold strawberry ice cream cones, and please put plenty of ice cream in them," said Uncle Wiggily to the man.

"Right you are!" cried the ice-cream-man in a jolly voice, and, say, I just wish you could have seen those cones! They were piled up heaping full of ice cream. Oh, my! It just makes me hungry to write about them.

Well, Uncle Wiggily, carefully carrying the cones, started to hop back to where he had left Grandfather Goosey. He hadn't gone far before he heard a growling voice cry out:

"Hold on there a moment, Uncle Wiggily!"

"Why?" asked the rabbit.

"Because I want to see what you've got," was the answer. "Ah, I see ice cream cones!" and with that a great, big, black bear jumped out of the bushes, and stood right in front of Uncle Wiggily.

"Let me pass!" cried the rabbit, holding the ice cream cones so that the bear couldn't get them.

"Indeed I will not!" cried the furry creature. "Ice cream cones, indeed! If there is one thing that I'm fonder of than another, ice cream cones is it! Let me taste one!"

Then before the rabbit could do anything, that bad bear took one ice cream cone right away from him. And that bear did more than that, so he did. He stuck his long, red tongue down inside the cone, and he licked out every bit of cream, with one, long lick.

"My but that's good!" he cried, smacking his lips. "I guess I'll try the second one," he said, and he dropped the empty cone, not eating it, mind you, and he took the other full cone away from poor Uncle Wiggily before the rabbit gentleman could stand on his head, or even wave his short tail.

"Oh, don't eat that cone. It belongs to Grandfather Goosey," cried the rabbit, sadlylike.

"Too late!" cried the bear, in a growlery voice. "Here it goes!" and with that he stuck his long, red tongue down inside the second cone, and with one lick he licked all the ice cream out and threw the empty cone on the ground.

"Now I feel good and hungry, and I guess I'll eat you," cried the bear. He made a grab for the poor gentleman rabbit, and folded him tight in his paws. But before that Uncle Wiggily had reached down and had picked up the two empty ice cream cones.

"Oh, let me go!" cried Uncle Wiggily to the bear.

"Indeed I'll not!" shouted the savage creature. "I want you for supper."

Well, he was just going to eat Uncle Wiggily up, when that brave rabbit just took the sharp points of those two empty ice cream cones, and he stuck them in the bear's ticklish ribs, and Uncle Wiggily tickled the bear so that the furry, savage creature sneezed out loud, and laughed so hard that Uncle Wiggily easily slipped out of his paws, and hopped away before he could be caught again.

So that's how the rabbit got safely away, and the empty ice cream cones were of some use after all. But Uncle Wiggily wondered how he could get a full one for Grandfather Goosey Gander, and how he did I'll tell you pretty soon, when, in case a butterfly doesn't bite a hole in my straw hat, the next story will be about Uncle Wiggily and the red ants.

Story XXVII

UNCLE WIGGILY AND THE RED ANTS

When Uncle Wiggily got to where Grandfather Goosey Gander was waiting for him, under the shady tree, the old gentleman duck jumped up and cried out:

"Oh, how glad I am to see you! I've just been wishing you would hurry back with those ice cream cones. My! I never knew the weather to be so warm at this time of the year. Oh, won't they taste most delicious — those cones!"

You see he didn't yet know what the bear had done — eaten all the ice cream out of the cones, as I told you in the other story.

"Oh, dear!" cried the rabbit. "How sorry I am to have to disappoint you, Grandfather, but there is no ice cream!"

"No ice cream!" cried the alligator — oh, dear me! I mean the duck. "No ice cream?"

"Not a bit," said Uncle Wiggily, and then he told about what the savage bear-creature had done, and also how he had used the cones to tickle him.

"Well, that's too bad," said Grandfather Goosey, "but here, I'll give you money to buy more cones with," and he put his hand in his pocket, but lo and behold! he had lost all his money.

"Never mind, perhaps *I* have some pennies," said the rabbit; so he looked, but, oh, dear me, suz-dud and the mustard pot! All of Uncle Wiggily's money was gone, too.

"Well, I guess we can't get any ice cream cones this week," said the old gentleman duck. "We'll have to drink water."

"Oh, no you won't," said a buzzing voice. "I'll get you each an ice cream cone, because you have always been so kind — both of you." And with that out from the bushes flew a big, sweet, honey bee, with a load of honey.

"Have you got any ice cream cones, Mr. Bee?" asked the rabbit.

"No, but I have sweet honey, and if I go down to the ice cream cone store, and give the man some of my honey he'll give me three cones, and there'll be one for you and one for me and —"

"One for Sister Sallie!" interrupted Grandfather Goosey. "I wish she was here now."

"She could have a cone if she was here," said the honey bee, "as I could get four. But, as long as she is not, the extra cone will go to you, Grandpa. Now, come on, and I'll take my honey to the ice-cream-cone-man."

So they went with him and on the way the bee sung a funny little song like this:

"I buzz, buzz, buzz
All day long.
I make my honey
Good and strong.

I fly about
To every flower
And sometimes stay
'Most half an hour."

Uncle Wiggily didn't know whether or not the bee was really in earnest about what he said, but, surely enough, when they got to the ice cream store, the man took the bee's honey, and handed out four ice cream cones, each larger than the first ones. Two were for the duck as he was so fond of them.

"Oh, let's eat them here, so that if the bear meets us he can't take them away," suggested Grandfather Goosey, and they did. Then the bee flew home to his hive, and Uncle Wiggily and the old gentleman duck found a nice place to sleep under a haystack.

In the morning Grandfather Goosey said he thought he had better go back home, as he had traveled enough. He wanted the rabbit to come with him, but Uncle Wiggily said:

"No, I have not yet found my fortune, and until I do I will keep on traveling." So he kept on, and the duck went home.

Well, it was about two days after that when, along toward evening, as Uncle Wiggily was walking down the road, he saw a real big house standing beside a lake. Oh, it was a very big house, about as big as a mountain, and the chimney on it was so tall as almost to reach the sky.

"Hum! I wonder who lives there?" said Uncle Wiggily. "Perhaps I can find my fortune in that house."

"Oh, no; never go there!" cried a voice down on the ground, and, looking toward his toes, Uncle Wiggily saw a little red ant.

"Ah, ha! Why shouldn't I go up to the big house, little red ant?" asked the rabbit.

"Because a monstrous giant lives there," was the answer, "and he could eat you up at one mouthful. So stay away."

"I guess I will," said the rabbit. "But I wonder where I can sleep tonight. I guess I'll go —"

"Oh, look out! Look out!" cried another red ant. "There is the giant coming now."

Uncle Wiggily looked, and he saw something like a big tree moving, and that was the giant. Then he felt the ground trembling as if a railroad train was rumbling past, and he heard a noise like thunder, and that was the giant walking and speaking:

"I smell rabbits! I smell rabbits!" cried the giant. "I must have them for supper!" Then he came on straight to where Uncle Wiggily was, but he hadn't yet seen him.

"Oh, what shall I do? What shall I do?" cried the bunny. "Let me hide behind that stone." He made a jump for a rock, taking his valise and crutch with him, but the first red ant said:

"It is no good hiding there, Uncle Wiggily, for the giant can see you."

"Oh, what shall I do?" he asked again, trembling with fear.

"I know!" cried the second little red ant. "Let's all bring grains of sand, and cover Uncle Wiggily up, leaving just a little hole for his nose, so he can breathe. Then the giant won't see him. It will be like down at the seashore, when they cover people on the beach up with the sand."

"Oh, it will take many grains of sand to cover the rabbit," said the first red ant, but still they were not discouraged. The first two ants called their brothers and sisters, and aunts, and uncles, and papas, and mammas, and cousins, and nephews, and forty-second granduncles. Soon there were twenty-two million four hundred and sixty-seven thousand, eight hundred and ninety-one ants, and a little baby ant, who counted as a half a one, and he carried baby grains of dirt.

Then each big ant took up a grain of sand, and then they all hurried up, and put them on Uncle Wiggily, who stretched out in the grass. Now all those ants together could carry lots of sand, you see, and soon the rabbit was completely buried from sight, all but the tip of his nose, so he could breathe, and when the giant came rumbling, stumbling by, he couldn't see the bunny, and so he didn't eat him. And, of course, the giant didn't eat the ants, either for he didn't like them.

"Hum! I thought I smelled a rabbit, but I guess I was mistaken," said the giant, grumbling and growling, as he tramped around.

And that's how Uncle Wiggily was saved, and pretty soon, if there isn't any sand in my rice pudding, I'll tell you about Uncle Wiggily and the bad giant.

Story XXVIII

UNCLE WIGGILY AND THE BAD GIANT

*D*o you remember about the giant, of whom I told you a little while ago, and how he couldn't find Uncle Wiggily, because the rabbit was covered with sand that the ants carried? Yes, I guess you do remember. Well, now I'm going to tell you what that giant did.

At first he was real surprised, because he couldn't find the bunny-rabbit, and he tramped around, making the ground shake with his heavy steps, and growling in his rumbling voice until you would have thought that it was thundering.

"My, my!" growled the giant. "To think that I can't have a rabbit supper after all. Oh, I'm so hungry that I could eat fourteen thousand, seven hundred and eighty-seven rabbits, and part of another one. But I guess I'll have to take a barrel of milk and a wagon load of crackers for my supper."

So that's what he did, and my how much he ate!

Well, after the giant had gone away, Uncle Wiggily crawled out from under the sand, and he said to the ants:

"I guess I'd better not stay around here, for it is too dangerous. I'll never find my fortune here, and if that giant were to see me he'd step on me, and make me as flat as a sheet of paper. I'm going."

"But wait," said the biggest ant of all. "You know there are two giants around here. One is a good one, and one is bad. Now if you go to the good giant I'm sure he will help you find your fortune."

"I'll try it," said the rabbit. "Where does the good giant live?"

"Just up the hill, in that house where you see the flag," said the big ant, as she ate two crumbs of bread and jam. "That's where the good giant lives. You must go where you see the fluttering flag, and you may find your fortune."

"I will," said Uncle Wiggily, "I'll go in the morning, the first thing after breakfast."

So the next morning he started off. But in the night something had happened and the rabbit didn't know a thing about it. After dark the bad giant got up, and he went over, and took the flag from the pole in front of the house of the good giant, and hoisted it up over his own house.

"I haven't any flag of my own," said the bad giant, "so I will take his." For you see, the two giants lived not far apart. In fact they were neighbors, but they were very different, one from the other, for one was kind and the other was cruel.

So it happened, that when Uncle Wiggily started to go to the giant's house he looked for the fluttering flag, and when he saw it on the bad giant's house he didn't know any better, but he thought it was the home of the good giant.

Well, the old gentleman rabbit walked on and on, having said good-bye to the ants, and pretty soon he was right close to the bad giant's house. But, all the while, he thought it was the good giant's place – so don't forget that.

"I wonder what sort of a fortune he'll give me," thought the rabbit. "I hope I soon get rich, so I can stop traveling, for I am tired."

Well, as he came near the place where the bad giant lived he heard a voice singing. And the song, which was sung in a deep, gruff, grumbling, growling voice, went something like this:

Oh, bing bang, bung!
Look out of the way for me.
For I'm so mad,
I feel so bad,
I could eat a hickory tree!

Oh, snip, snap, snoop!
Get off my big front stoop,
Or I'll tear my hair
In wild despair,
And burn you with hot soup!"

"My, that's a queer song for a good giant to sing," thought Uncle Wiggily. "But perhaps he just sings that for fun. I'm sure I'll find him a jolly enough fellow, when I get to know him."

Well, he went on a little farther, and pretty soon he came to the gate of the castle where the bad giant lived. The rabbit looked about, and saw no one there, so he kept right on, until, all of a sudden, he felt as if a big balloon had swooped down out of the sky, and had lifted him up. Higher and higher he went, until he found himself away up toward the roof of the castle, and then he looked and he saw two big fingers, about as big as a trolley car, holding him just as you would hold a bug.

"Oh, who has me?" cried Uncle Wiggily, very much frightened. "Let me go, please. Who are you?"

"I am the bad giant," was the answer, "and if I let you go now you'd fall to the ground and be killed. So I'll hold on to you."

"Are you the bad giant?" asked the rabbit. "Why, I thought I was coming to the good giant's house. Oh, please let me go!"

"No, I'm going to keep you," said the giant. "I just took the good giant's flag to fool you. Now, let me see, I think I'll just sprinkle sugar on you and eat you all up – no, I'll use salt – no, I think pepper would be better; I feel like pepper today."

So the bad giant started toward the cupboard to get the pepper caster, and poor Uncle Wiggily thought it was all up with him.

"Oh, I wish I'd never thought of coming to see any giant, good or bad," the rabbit gentleman said. "Now good-bye to all my friends!"

"Hum! Let me see," spoke the bad giant, standing still. "Pepper – no, I think I'll put some mustard on you – no, I'll try ketchup – no, I mean horseradish. Oh, dear, I can't seem to make up my mind what to flavor you with," and he held Uncle Wiggily there in his fingers, away up about a hundred feet high in the air, and wondered what he'd do with the old gentleman rabbit.

And it's a good thing he didn't eat him right away, for that was the means of saving Uncle Wiggily's life. Right after breakfast the good giant found out that his bad neighbor had taken his flag, so he went and told the ants all about it.

"Oh, then Uncle Wiggily must have been mixed up about the flag, and he has gone to the wrong place, and he'll be eaten," said the big ant. "We must save him. Come on, everybody!"

So all the ants hurried along together, and crawled to the castle of the bad giant, and they got there just as he was putting some molasses on Uncle Wiggily to eat him. And those ants crawled all over the giant, on his legs and arms, and nose and ears and toes, and they tickled him so that he squiggled and wiggled and squirreled and whirled, and finally he let Uncle Wiggily fall on a feather bed, not hurting him a bit, and the rabbit gentleman hopped safely away and the ants crawled with him far from the castle of the bad giant.

So Uncle Wiggily was saved by the ants, and in case the trolley car doesn't run over my stick of peppermint candy, and make it look like a lollypop, I'll tell you soon about Uncle Wiggily and the good giant.

Story XXIX

UNCLE WIGGILY AND THE GOOD GIANT

*N*ow what do you s'pose that bad giant had for supper the night after the ants helped Uncle Wiggily get away? You'd never guess, so I'll tell you. It was beans — just baked beans, and that giant was so disappointed, and altogether so cut-up about not having rabbit stew, that he ate so many beans, that I'm almost afraid to tell you just how many.

But if all the boys in your school were to take their bean shooters, and shoot beans out of a bag for a million years, and Fourth of July also, that giant could eat all of them, and more too — that is, if he could get the beans after the boys shot them away.

"Well, I certainly must be more careful after this," said Uncle Wiggily to the ants, as they crawled along down the hill with him, when he hopped away from the bad giant's house.

"Oh, it wasn't your fault," said the second size big red ant, with black and yellow stripes on his stockings. "That bad giant changed the flags, and that's what fooled you. But I guess the good giant will have his flag back by tomorrow, and then you can go to the right house. We'll go along and show you, and you may get your fortune from him."

So, surely enough, the next day, the good giant went over and took his flag away from the bad giant, and put it upon his own house.

"Now you'll be all right," said the pink ant, with purple spots on his necktie. "You won't make any mistake now, Uncle Wiggily. I'm sure the good giant will give you a good fortune."

"Yes, and he'll give you lots to eat," said the black ant with white rings around his nose.

Well, Uncle Wiggily took his valise and his crutch and up toward the good giant's house he went, with the ants crawling along in the sand to show him the way.

Pretty soon they came to a big bridge, over a stream of water, and this was the beginning of the place where the good giant lived.

"We'll all have to go back now," said the purple ant, with the green patchwork squares on his checks. "If we crossed over the bridge we might fall off and be drowned. We'll go back, but you go ahead, and we wish you good luck, Uncle Wiggily."

"Indeed we do," said a white ant with gold buckles on her shoes.

Well, after a little while Uncle Wiggily found himself right inside the good giant's house. And oh! what a big place it was. Why, even the door mat was so big that it took the rabbit three hops to get to the top of it. And that front door! I wish you could have seen it! It was as large as one of your whole houses, and it was only a door, mind you.

"Hello! hello!" cried Uncle Wiggily, as he pounded with his crutch on the floor. "Is anyone at home?"

"But no one answered, and there wasn't a sound except the ticking of the clock, and that made as much noise as a railroad train going over a bridge, for the clock was a big as a church steeple.

"Hum! No one is home," said Uncle Wiggily. "I'll just sit down and make myself comfortable." So he sat down on the floor by the table that was away over his head, and waited for the giant to come back.

And, all of a sudden, the rabbit heard a noise like a steam engine going, and he was quite surprised, until he happened to look up, and there stood a pussy cat as big as a cow, and the cat was purring, which made the noise like a steam engine.

"My, if that's the size of the cat, what must the giant be," thought the rabbit. "I do hope he's good-natured when he comes home."

Well, pretty soon, in a little while, as Uncle Wiggily was sitting there, listening to the big cat purr, he felt sleepy, and he was just going to sleep, when he heard a gentle voice singing:

"Oh, see the blackbird, sitting in the tree,
Hear him singing, jolly as can be.
Now he'll whistle a pretty little tune,
Isn't it delicious in the month of June?

"Hear the bees a-buzzing, hour by hour,
Gathering the honey from every little flower.
The katydid is singing by his own front door,
Now I'll have to stop this song — I don't know anymore."

"Well, whoever that is, he's a jolly chap," said the rabbit, and with that who should come in but the giant himself.

"Ho! Ho! Whom have we here?" the giant asked, looking at Uncle Wiggily. "What do you want, my little furry friend with the long ears? You must be able to hear very well with them."

"I can hear pretty well," said the rabbit. "But I came to seek my fortune."

"Fine," cried the good giant, for he it was. "I'll do all I can for you," and he laughed so long and hard that part of the ceiling and the gas chandelier fell down, but the giant caught them in his strong hands, and not even the pussy cat was hurt. Then the giant sung another song, like the first, only different, and he fixed the broken ceiling, and said:

"Now for something to eat! Then we'll talk about your fortune. I'll get you some carrots." So he went out, and pretty soon he came back, carrying ten barrels of carrots in one hand and seventeen bushels of cabbage in the other.

"Here's a little light lunch for you," he said to Uncle Wiggily. "Eat this, and I'll get you some more, when we have a regular meal."

"Oh, why this is more than I could eat in a year," said the rabbit, "but I thank you very much," so he nibbled at one carrot, while the good giant ate fifteen thousand seven hundred and eight loaves of bread, and two million bushels of jam. Then he felt better.

"So you want to find your fortune, eh?" the giant said to the rabbit. "Well, now I'll help you all I can. How would you like to stay here and work for me? You have good ears, and you could listen for burglars in the night when I am asleep. Will you?"

"I think I will," said Uncle Wiggily. And he was just reaching for another carrot, when suddenly from outside sounded a terrible racket.

"Where is he? Let me get at him! I want him right away — that rabbit I mean!" cried a voice, and Uncle Wiggily jumped up in great fright, and looked for some place to hide. The giant jumped up, too, and grabbed his big club.

But don't be alarmed. Nothing bad is going to happen to our Uncle Wiggily — in fact he is going to have lots of fun soon.

So if my motorboat doesn't turn upside down and spill out the pink lemonade, I'll tell you in the next story about Uncle Wiggily and the giant's little boy.

Story XXX

UNCLE WIGGILY AND THE GIANT'S BOY

Let me see, I believe I left off where Uncle Wiggily was in the house of the good giant, and the old gentleman rabbit heard a terrible noise. Didn't I?

"My goodness!" exclaimed the rabbit, jumping up so quickly that he upset one of the giant's toothpicks, on which he had been sitting for a chair, for the giant's toothpicks were as large as a big chestnut tree. "My goodness!" cried Uncle Wiggily, "what in the world is that?"

"I guess it's my little boy coming home from school," said the good giant as softly as he could, but, even then, his voice was like thunder. "He must have heard that you were here."

"Will he hurt me? Does he love animals?" asked the rabbit, for he was getting frightened. "Will your little boy be kind to me?"

"Oh, indeed he will!" cried the good giant. "I have taught him to love animals, for you know he is so big and strong, even though I do call him my *little* boy, that it would be no trouble for him to take a bear or a lion, and squeeze him in one hand so that the bear or lion would never hurt anyone anymore. But, just because he is big and strong, though not so big and strong as I am, I have taught my boy to be kind to the little animals."

"Then I will have no fear," said Uncle Wiggily, winking his nose – I mean his eyes – and just then the door of the giant's house opened and in came his little boy.

Well, at first Uncle Wiggily was so frightened that he did not know what to do. I wonder what you would say if you were suddenly to see a boy almost as big as your house, or mine, walk into the parlor, and sit down at the piano? Well, that's what the old gentleman rabbit saw.

"Ah, my little boy is home from school," said the giant, kindly. "Did you have your lessons, my son?"

"Yes, father, I did," was the answer. "And I learned a new song. I'll sing it for you."

So he began to play the piano with his little finger nail, and still, and with all that, he made as much noise as a circus band of music can make on a hot day in the tent. Oh, he played terribly loud, the giant's boy did, and Uncle Wiggily had to put his paws over his ears, or he might have been made deaf. Then the giant's little boy sang, and even when he hummed it the noise was like a thunder storm, only different. Now, this is the boy giant's song, and you will have to sing it with all your might, as hard as you can, but not if the baby is asleep.

"I am a little fellow,
  But soon I will grow big.
And then I'll sit beside the sea,
And in the white sand dig.

"I'll make a hole so very deep,
  To China it will go.
And then I'll fill it up with shells
Wherein the wild waves blow."

And with that the giant's little boy banged so hard on the piano with his little finger nail that he broke a string, and made a funny sound, like a banjo out of tune.

"Oh, I didn't mean to do that!" the giant's boy cried. "I'm sorry!"

"Dear me! I wonder when you'll grow up?" asked the giant, sort of sadlike.

"I think he's pretty big now," said Uncle Wiggily. And, indeed, the boy-giant was so tall that when the rabbit stood up as high as he could stand, he only came up to the tip end of the shoe laces on the giant boy's big shoes.

"Oh, he grows very slowly," said the giant, and then the boy noticed the rabbit for the first time. Well, that boy-giant wanted to know all about Uncle Wiggily, where he came from and where he was going, and all that, and Uncle Wiggily told about how he was traveling around to seek his fortune.

"Oh, I believe I know where you can find lots of money, Uncle Wiggily," said the giant's boy kindly, as he reached over and stroked the rabbit's ears. "I have always heard that there is a pot of gold at the end of the rainbow. The next time we see one, you and I will go out and search for the money. Then you will have your fortune, and you won't have to travel around anymore."

"That will be fine!" cried the rabbit, "for, to tell you the truth, I am getting pretty tired of going about the country. Still, I will not give up until I find my fortune."

"All right. But we will have to wait until it rains, and then we'll see where the end of the rainbow is," said the giant's boy. "Now we will have some games together. Let's play tag."

Well, they started to play that, but, land's sake, flopsy dub and a basket of ice cream cones! Uncle Wiggily ran here, and there, and everywhere, and he jumped and leaped about so that the giant's little boy couldn't catch him, for the big-little fellow wasn't very spry on his feet.

"Oh, I guess we had better not play that game anymore," said the boy giant, as he accidentally nearly stepped on Uncle Wiggily's left ear. "I might hurt you. Let's play hide-and-go-seek."

But Uncle Wiggily was even better at this game than he had been at tag, for he could hide in such small holes that the boy giant couldn't even see them, so of course that wouldn't do for a game. It was no fun.

Then all at once it began to rain. My! how it did pour! It rained snips and snails and puppy dogs' tails, with the puppies fast to the tails, of course, and the streets were covered with them. Then it rained a few ice cream cones, and Uncle Wiggily and the giant boy had all they wanted to eat, the giant eating fourteen thousand seven hundred and eighty-six, and part of another one, while Uncle Wiggily had only two cones.

"Oh, there is the rainbow!" cried the boy giant at last, as he saw the beautiful gold and green and orange and red colors in the sky. "Now for the pot of gold."

So he and Uncle Wiggily started off together to find it. But they had not gone very far through the woods before they met the papa giant.

"Where are you going?" he asked of them.

"To the end of the rainbow to get the pot of gold," said the giant's little boy.

"You don't need to," said the giant, "for there is none there. That is only a fairy story. Wait, I'll show you."

So he stretched out his long arm as far as it would go and he reached away down to the end of the rainbow and he felt all around with his long fingers, and sure enough, there wasn't a bit of gold there, for his hand came back empty.

"It's too bad," said the giant's little boy to Uncle Wiggily. "There is nothing there for you. But perhaps you will find your fortune tomorrow. Come and stay with me until morning."

So Uncle Wiggily went back to the giant's house, and the next day quite a surprising adventure occurred to him, and in case the gasoline in my motorboat doesn't wash all the paint off my red necktie I'll tell you next about Uncle Wiggily and Grand-daddy Longlegs.

Story XXXI

UNCLE WIGGILY AND DADDY LONGLEGS

*U*ncle Wiggily got up early the morning after the good giant had shown him that there wasn't any gold at the end of the rainbow. The old gentleman rabbit looked where a place had been set for him at the table, but alas and alack a-day, the table was almost as high from the floor as the church steeple is from the ground, and Uncle Wiggily could not reach up to it.

"Hum, let's see what we will do," spoke the papa giant. "I know, I'll get a spool of thread from the lady giant next door, and that will answer for a table for you, Uncle Wiggily, and you can use another toothpick for a chair."

So while the boy giant went for the spool of thread, the papa giant served Uncle Wiggily's breakfast. First he brought in a washtub full of milk and a bushel basket full of oatmeal.

"What is that for?" asked the rabbit in surprise.

"That is for your breakfast," was the answer. "Isn't it enough? Because I can get you more in a jiffy, if you want it."

"Oh, it is entirely too much," said Uncle Wiggily. "I can only take a little of that oatmeal."

"Very well, then, I will take this myself, and get you a small dish full," spoke the papa giant, and he ate all that oatmeal and milk up at one mouthful, but even then it was hardly enough to fill his hollow tooth.

Then the boy giant came back with the spool, which was as big as the dining room table in a rabbit's house. Up at this new table the traveling uncle sat, and he ate a very good breakfast indeed.

"Now I must start off again to seek my fortune," he said, as he took his crutch, striped red, green and yellow, like a cow's horn. Oh, excuse me! I was thinking of circus balloons, I guess. Anyhow Uncle Wiggily took his crutch and valise, and, as he was about to start off, the boy giant said:

"I will walk along a short distance with you, and in case any bad animals try to hurt you I'll drive them away."

"Oh, I don't believe anyone will harm me," spoke the rabbit, but nevertheless something did happen to him. As he and the boy giant were walking along, all of a sudden there was a noise from behind a big, black stump, and out jumped a big, black bear. He rushed right at the rabbit, and called out:

"Ha! Now I have you! I've been waiting a long while for you, and I thought you'd never come. But, better late than never. Now for my dinner! I've had the fire made for some time to cook you, and the kettle is boiling for tea." He was just going to grab our Uncle Wiggily, when the giant's little boy called out:

"Here, you let that rabbit alone! He's a friend of mine!" But, listen to this, the bear never thought a thing about a boy giant being with Uncle Wiggily, and he never even looked up at him. Only when the bear heard the giant's boy speaking he thought it was distant thunder, and he said:

"Oh, I must hurry home with that rabbit before it rains. I don't like to get wet!"

"Yes, I guess you *will* hurry home!" cried the giant's boy, and with that he reached over, and he grabbed that black, ugly bear by his short, stumpy tail and he flung him away over the tree tops, like a skyrocket, and it was some time before that bear came down. And when he did, he didn't feel like bothering Uncle Wiggily anymore.

"Now I guess you'll be all right for a while on your travels," said the boy giant as he called good-bye to the old gentleman rabbit. "Send me a souvenir postal when you find your fortune, and if any bad animals bother you, just telephone for me, and I'll come and serve them as I did the bear."

Then the old gentleman rabbit thanked the boy giant, and started off again. He traveled on and on, over hills and down in little valleys, and across brooks that flowed over green mossy stones in the meadow, and pretty soon Uncle Wiggily came to a big grey stone in the middle of a field. And, as he looked at the stone, the old gentleman rabbit saw something red fluttering behind it, and he heard a noise like someone crying.

"Ha! Here is where I must be careful!" exclaimed the rabbit to himself. "Perhaps that is a red fox behind the stone, and he is making believe cry, so as to bring me up close, and then he'll jump out and grab me. No indeed, I'm going to run back."

Well, Uncle Wiggily was just going to run back, when he happened to look again, and there, instead of a fox behind the stone, it was a little boy, with red trousers on, and he was crying as hard as he could cry, that boy was.

"What is the matter, my little chap?" asked the rabbit kindly. "Are you crying because you have on red trousers instead of blue? I think red is a lovely color myself. I wish I had red ears, as well as red eyes."

"Oh, I am not crying for that," said the little boy, wiping away his tears on a big green leaf, "but you see I am like Bo-peep, only I have lost my cows, instead of my sheep, and I don't know where to find them."

"Oh, I'll help you look," said Uncle Wiggily. "I am pretty good at finding lost cows. Come, we'll hunt farther." So off they started together, Uncle Wiggily holding the little boy by one of his paws — one of the rabbit's paws, I mean.

Well, they looked and looked, but they couldn't seem to find those cows. They looked at one hill, and on top of another hill, and down in the hollows, and under the trees by the brook, but no cows were to be seen.

"Oh, dear!" cried the little boy, "if I don't find them soon there'll be no milk for dinner."

"And I am very thirsty, too," said the rabbit. "I wish I had a drink of milk. But where in the world can those cows be?" and he looked up into the sky, not because he thought the cows were there, but so that he might think better. Then he looked down at the ground, and, as he did so he saw a little red creature with eight long legs, and the creature wiggled one leg at the rabbit friendlylike as if to shake hands.

"Why don't you ask me where the cows are?" said the long-legged insect.

"Why, can you tell?" inquired Uncle Wiggily.

"Of course I can. I'm a grand-daddy longlegs, and I can always tell where the cows are," was the reply. "Just you ask me."

So Uncle Wiggily and the little boy, both together, politely asked where they could find the cows, and the grand-daddy just pointed with one long leg off toward the woods where the rabbit and boy hadn't thought of looking before that.

"You'll find your cows there," said grand-daddy longlegs, and then he hurried home to his dinner. And Uncle Wiggily and the boy went over to the woods, and there in the shade by a brook — sure enough were the cows, chewing their gum — I mean their cuds. And they were just waiting to be driven home.

So Uncle Wiggily, and the boy with the red trousers, drove the cows home, and they were milked, and the old gentleman rabbit had several glasses full — glasses full of milk, not cows, you know. Goodness me! A cow couldn't get into a glass could it? I guess not!

And after that Uncle Wiggily –

Well, but see here now. I think I've put enough adventures about Uncle Wiggily in this book, and I must save some for another one. So I think I will call the following book "Uncle Wiggily's Travels," for he still kept on traveling after his fortune you know. And he found it, too, which is the best part of it. Oh, my yes! He found his fortune all right. Don't worry about that. And in the next book, the very first thing he did, was to have an adventure with a red squirrel-girl, who was some relation to Johnnie and Billie Bushytail.

So that's all there is to Uncle Wiggily, for a little while, if you please, but if you want to hear anything else about him I'll try, later on, to tell you some more stories. And now, dear children, good-bye.

THE END

CPSIA information can be obtained at www.ICGtesting.com
Printed in the USA
LVOW13*1408260214

375264LV00002B/14/P